Bob and Pete silently followed Jupe into the grove of dark trees. What strange rites of witchcraft were they about to witness?

The boys spied three figures wearing long black robes, standing in a ring of eerie, flickering candlelight. A woman with ghostly white-blond hair lifted a cup high and closed her eyes. Was she praying to some unnatural spirit?

Suddenly Pete felt a hot breath on his skin!

Had the witch summoned an evil spirit to attack the boys?

The Mystery of the Magic Circle

The Three Investigators in

The Mystery of the Magic Circle

By M. V. Carey
Based on characters created by Robert Arthur

Random House 🏠 New York

Originally published by Random House in 1978.
First Random House paperback edition, 1981.
Revised edition, 1985.

Library of Congress Cataloging in Publication Data:
Carey, M. V.
  The Three Investigators in The mystery of the magic circle.
  (The Three Investigators mystery series ; 27)
  SUMMARY: Three young sleuths uncover a coven of witches when
they search for the missing memoirs of a movie star.
  [1. Mystery and detective stories. 2. Witchcraft—Fiction]
I. Arthur, Robert.   II. Title.   III. Title: Mystery of the magic circle.
IV. Series.
PZ7.C213Tgk 1985   [Fic]   83-27080
ISBN: 0-394-86427-1 (pbk.)

Manufactured in the United States of America
      3 4 5 6 7 8 9 0

Contents

A Word from
Hector Sebastian

Hello, mystery lovers! It's again my privilege to introduce another adventure of The Three Investigators, my fearless young friends whose specialty is mystery—and the more bizarre the mystery, the better. In the story that follows, the junior detectives come up against a witch who hides from the world, practicing secret rites and brooding over an accident that happened long ago. Or was it an accident? Some people think it was murder done by magic.

If you've already met The Three Investigators, you can skip the rest of this introduction. If not, let me tell you a little about them. Jupiter Jones, the leader of the group, is called stocky by some people and called fat by others. But everyone agrees that he's a whiz at deduction. Jupiter's enthusiasm for solving puzzles often gets the boys into tight corners. That sometimes unnerves Pete Crenshaw, the Second Investigator, though Pete can always be counted on to overcome his doubts and help out his fellow Investigators. Pete is the tallest and most athletic of the three. Bob Andrews uses his talent for research to scour up background information for the problems the boys encounter. Bob also keeps the firm's records. All three boys live in the town of Rocky Beach, California, which is on the Pacific Coast, close to Hollywood.

If you're wondering how I fit into this, I'll briefly say that I'm a mystery writer who had the good luck to meet the boys over a case. When they solved it, I started introducing their cases for them. And now— get set for a story about modern-day witchcraft. If you don't believe in magic—as I didn't—you're in for a surprise.

HECTOR SEBASTIAN

The Mystery of
the Magic Circle

1

Fire!

"Exactly what are you boys up to?" demanded Horace Tremayne. He stood in the doorway of the mail room of Amigos Press and scowled at Jupiter Jones, Bob Andrews, and Pete Crenshaw.

"Up to?" said Pete. "We're . . . we're just sorting the mail."

"Don't give me that!" snapped Tremayne. His face, which was usually quite pleasant, looked threatening. "You've got some nerve, pretending to be mail clerks when you're really private detectives!"

With that, Tremayne—the young man who was publisher at Amigos Press, and who was called Beefy by everyone on the staff—relaxed and began to chuckle. "You *are* private detectives, aren't you?" he said.

"Hey," said Pete, "you really scared me!"

Bob Andrews smiled. "The private detective business is slow this summer," he said. "We thought we'd get some experience with office work."

"How did you find out about us?" asked Jupiter Jones, his round faced filled with curiosity.

"Last night my uncle Will hired a limousine to take us to a premiere in Hollywood," said Beefy Tremayne. "It was a gold-plated Rolls-Royce, driven by a British chauffeur named Worthington."

"I see." Jupe laughed, for Worthington was an old friend. Some time before, Jupe had entered a contest sponsored by the Rent-'n-Ride Auto Rental Company and had won the use of the gold-plated Rolls for thirty days. Worthington had chauffeured the car for the boys, and had become fascinated with their detective work.

"Your names came up when Worthington started telling me about his regular clients," Beefy explained. "When he heard that you three had summer jobs here, he said I was in for a lively time. He said that trouble just seems to happen when you're around."

"It doesn't just seem to happen," said Pete. "Jupe stirs it up!"

"Then we all help settle it," put in Bob.

Jupiter took a card from his wallet and handed it to Beefy. It read:

THE THREE INVESTIGATORS
"We Investigate Anything"
?   ?   ?

First Investigator . . . . Jupiter Jones
Second Investigator . . . . Pete Crenshaw
Records and Research . . . . Bob Andrews

"Very professional," said Beefy. "What are the question marks for?"

The stocky First Investigator looked smug. People always asked about the question marks. "They're the universal symbol of the unknown," said Jupe. "The unknown is always intriguing."

"Yes, it is," agreed Beefy. "If I ever need a private detective firm, I might call you. Worthington says you're very clever."

"We've been able to solve a number of interesting cases," said Jupe. "We think our success is due to the fact that we believe almost anything can happen."

"You're young enough not to be prejudiced, eh?" Beefy commented. "That could be a great help in an investigation. Too bad there's nothing around here that needs investigating—besides why the coffee machine makes such lousy coffee!"

The boys heard footsteps outside the mail room. Beefy stepped back into the hall and looked toward the front of the building. "Uncle Will, what took you so long?" he called.

A second later, a tall, thin man with sandy hair and a small mustache appeared beside Beefy. He was Mr. William Tremayne and, as usual, he looked very elegant. He wore beige slacks and a linen jacket the color of cocoa. He glanced into the mail room but didn't bother to speak to the boys.

"They didn't have a loaner when I left the car at the garage," he told his nephew. "I had to call a cab. It's so tiresome. Nothing is really properly organized these days."

"I suppose not," said Beefy in his cheerful way. "Say,

listen, Uncle Will, today's the day Marvin Gray's coming in with that manuscript. Do you want to see him about anything when he gets here?"

"Marvin Gray?" William Tremayne looked both bored and puzzled.

"Oh, come on, Uncle Will, you remember him," said Beefy. "He's Madeline Bainbridge's business manager. He negotiated the contract for her book."

"Ah, yes," said William Tremayne. "The chauffeur."

"He *used* to be her chauffeur." Beefy sounded irritated, but he took a deep breath and kept his voice level. "He's Bainbridge's business manager now, and that manuscript he's bringing could be terrific. Madeline Bainbridge knew everybody who was anybody in Hollywood when she was a star. Just wait till the news gets out that we're going to publish her memoirs!"

"I'm sure it will cause a sensation," said Will Tremayne disdainfully. "I do not understand this fascination with has-been actresses, but there is no reason why we shouldn't make money on it."

"Bainbridge isn't a has-been," said Beefy.

"Then what is she?" demanded his uncle. "She hasn't made a picture for thirty years."

"She's a legend," Beefy declared.

"Is there a difference?" asked William Tremayne. He turned away without waiting for an answer. A moment later the boys heard him on the stairs that led up to the second floor, where he had his office. Beefy stood looking unhappy, as he often did after an exchange with his uncle.

"Have you actually met Madeline Bainbridge?" Jupe asked.

Beefy blinked. "You know about her?"

"I'm a student of films and the theater," Jupe explained. "I've read about her. She was beautiful, and supposedly also a fine actress. Of course, it's hard to judge today, when her films are never in release or on television."

"I haven't actually met her," said Beefy. "She's a recluse. She doesn't see anyone. She does everything through Marvin Gray. He seems a very competent business manager, even if he did start out as a chauffeur. Bainbridge bought the negatives of her films from the producers when she retired, and they're in storage in a special vault on her estate near Malibu. Marvin Gray hinted that she may sell them to television soon. If she does, her book could be the best-seller of the year."

Beefy grinned at the thought, and left the mail room. The boys heard him start up the stairs and stumble. He recovered and climbed to the second floor, whistling cheerfully.

"He's a nice guy," said Pete, "but he's got no coordination."

No one argued with this. The boys had been working in the offices of Amigos Press for three weeks, and they knew that Beefy Tremayne tripped on the stairs every morning. He was as broad shouldered and muscular as any athlete, but he gave the impression of being made of slightly mismatched parts. His legs were just a bit too short to go with his barrel chest. His feet were slightly too small, and so was his nose, which he had fallen on and broken at some time in his life, so that now it was flattened and slightly crooked. His fair hair was cropped close, yet it managed to seem untidy. And although his clothes were always fresh and starched, they were also always somewhat rumpled. He was homely, and yet very pleasant looking. The boys liked him.

Pete and Bob began sorting the mail into neat stacks on the long table that ran along one side of the room. Jupe was just opening a big canvas sack stuffed with letters when a withered-looking, gray-haired man came bustling in.

"Good morning, Mr. Grear," said Jupiter.

"Morning, Jupe," he replied. "Morning, Bob. Pete."

Mr. Grear, who was the office manager, went into the small room that adjoined the mail room and sat down at his desk. "Have you seen Mr. William Tremayne this morning?" he asked.

"He went upstairs a few minutes ago," said Jupe.

"I have to see him," said Mr. Grear. He sighed. Mr. Grear was not fond of William Tremayne. Indeed, no one on the staff seemed to care for him. William Tremayne was regarded as a usurper. Amigos Press had been founded by Beefy's father, and Beefy was heir to it. A tragic boating accident had made Beefy an orphan when he was nineteen, but according to the terms of the will left by Beefy's father, William Tremayne was president of Amigos Press and would control the business until Beefy was thirty.

"I guess Beefy's father only meant to protect Beefy and his inheritance," Mr. Grear had said one day. "He was such a clumsy boy. No one suspected that he'd show a flair for publishing, but he did. He's got a real nose for a salable manuscript. Now, in spite of that, we're all stuck with William Tremayne—at least until next April, when Beefy turns thirty. It's a great trial. He's the only one who can make any decisions about money, so every time I need new supplies—even a box of pencils—I have to get his permission to order them!"

Mr. Grear always looked outraged when he told the boys about William Tremayne. He looked outraged now, but he did not speak again. He was still in his office, staring unhappily at the papers on his desk, when Pete set out to deliver the mail to the other offices in the building.

Amigos Press was located in the Amigos Adobe, a historic two-story structure that was sandwiched between more modern commercial buildings on busy Pacifica Avenue in Santa Monica. The adobe dated back to the days when California was ruled by governors from Mexico. The walls were thick, as adobe walls always are, and even though the summer sun blazed outside, the rooms were cool. Decorative iron grilles on all the first-floor windows added to the charm of the building.

Pete stopped first in the accounting department, a big room across the hall from the mail room. A dour, middle-aged man headed this department, supervising the work of two sullen women who labored there with adding machines and heaps of invoices.

"Good morning, Mr. Thomas," said Pete. He put a packet of envelopes down on the man's desk.

Thomas scowled. "Put the mail in the box on that table over there," he ordered. "What's the matter with you? Can't you remember a simple thing like that?"

"All right, Thomas," said a voice behind Pete. It

was Mr. Grear. He had come out into the hall and was watching Mr. Thomas. "I'm sure Pete understands. Just remember, *I* supervise the mail room. If the boys get out of line, you tell me and *I'll* talk to them."

Pete scooted out of the accounting department. As he passed Mr. Grear in the hall, he heard the office manager muttering to himself. "Troublemaker! He won't last a year here. I don't know how they put up with him at that pharmaceutical company for five years!"

Pete didn't comment. He had several letters for the receptionist, whose desk was in the big front room of the adobe. He delivered these, and then went up the stairs to the second floor. The editors, book designers, and production people had offices there.

Mr. Grear and Mr. Thomas did not speak to each other again until midafternoon. Then the copying machine that stood in a corner of the mail room jammed. This caused a fierce argument between Mr. Thomas, who insisted that the machine be fixed immediately, and Mr. Grear, who declared that the serviceman couldn't come until morning.

The two men were still exchanging angry words when Jupiter went upstairs shortly before four to collect outgoing mail from the staff there. Mrs. Paulson, Beefy's assistant, looked up and smiled when Jupe stopped at her desk. She was a smooth-faced, plump woman many years Beefy's senior, who had previously been assistant to Beefy's father. She handed a couple of envelopes to Jupe. Then she glanced past him at someone just coming up the stairs.

"He's waiting for you," she said, pointing to the open door of Beefy's office.

Jupe looked around. A thin, dark-haired man in a light gabardine suit went past him and into Beefy's office.

"That's Marvin Gray," said Mrs. Paulson softly. "He's delivering Madeline Bainbridge's manuscript." Mrs. Paulson sighed. "He's given his whole life to looking after Madeline Bainbridge. Isn't that romantic?"

Before Jupe could comment, Beefy came out of his office with a sheaf of papers in his hands. "Oh, Jupe, I'm glad you're here," he said. "Take this manuscript down to the copying machine and make a duplicate of it right away. It's handwritten, and there's no copy. Mr. Gray is concerned about its safety."

"The machine is out of order," said Jupe. "Shall I take the manuscript out to a service?"

Gray appeared in the doorway beside Beefy. "No, don't do that," he said. "It would be safer just to keep it here."

"We'll take good care of it," promised Beefy.

Gray nodded. "Fine. And now that you have the manuscript, if you'll give me the check, I'll be on my way."

"The check?" Beefy echoed. "You mean the advance?"

"Why, yes," said Gray. "According to the contract, you are to pay Miss Bainbridge twenty-five thousand dollars upon delivery of the manuscript."

Beefy looked flustered. "Mr. Gray, we usually read

the manuscript first. The check hasn't even been made out yet."

"Oh," said Marvin Gray. "I see. All right. I'll look forward to receiving the check in the mail."

He went off then, down the stairs.

"He's certainly in a hurry for the money," said Mrs. Paulson.

"I guess he doesn't understand publishing contracts," said Beefy. "He missed the phrase about how the manuscript has to be acceptable."

Beefy went back into his office and Jupe returned to the mail room.

"Want to work overtime tonight?" Mr. Grear said when Jupe came in. "The printer just sent over the brochures for the mailing on the songbird book. We can stuff the envelopes in a couple of hours, and I can take them to the post office first thing in the morning."

The boys were glad to put in the extra time, and they called their homes in Rocky Beach to report that they would be home late. They were busy folding circulars and putting them into envelopes when the rest of the staff left, singly and in groups. At a quarter to six, Mr. Grear set out to take the last of the mail to the main post office. "On my way back I'll pick up some fried chicken at the shop down the street," he promised.

The boys toiled on after he left. A breeze came up and blew through the open window of the mail room. It caught at the door and slammed it shut. The boys jumped at the sound, then resumed work.

It was six-fifteen when Bob stopped working and sniffed. "Do I smell smoke?" he said.

Pete looked around at the closed door. In the silence, the boys heard the hum of traffic on Pacifica Avenue. They heard another sound, too—a low, crackling roar that came to them muffled by the thick adobe walls.

Jupe frowned. He went to the door and put his hand against it. The wood felt warm. He put his hand on the knob, which felt even warmer, and very cautiously pulled the door open.

Instantly the roar became almost deafening. A great billow of smoke gushed into the room and overwhelmed the boys.

"Good grief!" shouted Pete.

Jupe threw his weight against the door and slammed it shut. He turned to face the others. "The hall!" he said. "There's fire all over the hall!"

The smoke was seeping in around the door now, thickening the air as it wafted toward the open window, which looked out on a narrow walkway between the adobe and the building next door. He leaned on the iron grillwork covering the window and pushed. "Help!" he shouted. "Help! Fire!"

No one answered and the bars didn't budge.

Bob snatched up a metal chair and shoved it through the bars. He and Pete tried to pry the metal grille away from the building. The chair only bent in their hands, and one leg snapped off.

"It's no use," called Jupe from Mr. Grear's office. "The telephone is dead. And there's no one around to hear us yell."

He hurried back to the door that led to the hall. "We've got to get ourselves out, and this is the only way."

He went down on his knees, and again he edged the door open. Again the smoke gushed in through the opening. Bob coughed, and Pete's eyes began streaming. The two boys knelt behind Jupe and peered out into the hall. They saw smoke that looked almost solid. It seethed and glowed red with the light of flames that danced up the walls and licked away at the old staircase.

Jupe turned his face from the fire for an instant. He took a breath that was almost a sob. Then he started forward, holding his breath. But before he could get through the doorway, a gust of hot air pushed at him like a giant hand. He flinched, drew back, and slammed the door.

"We can't," he whispered. "Nobody can go through that fire! There's no way out! We're trapped!"

2

The Bleeding Man

For a moment no one spoke. Then Pete made a choking sound. "Someone's got to see the smoke and call the fire department," he gasped. "Someone's just *got* to!"

Jupe looked around wildly. For the first time he saw something that might give them a chance. There was a trap door under the long table that the boys used for wrapping and sorting.

Jupe pointed. "Look! There must be a cellar. The air's bound to be better down there."

The boys ran to pull the table away from the wall. Pete pried open the trap door, and they looked down into a brick-walled cellar. Its dirt floor was more than eight feet beneath them, and they smelled air that was heavy with damp and decay. The boys didn't hesitate. Pete swung down through the trap-door opening, holding on to the edge of the floor, then let himself

15

drop the few remaining feet. The others followed. When they were safely in the cellar, Bob stood on Pete's shoulders and pulled the trap door shut.

The boys stood in the darkness and strained to listen. They could still hear the fire. They were safe, but for how long? In his mind's eye Jupe pictured flames mushrooming through the second floor and eating away at the roof. What if the roof caved in? Would the floor above them hold if flaming timbers came crashing down on it? Even if it did hold, would anyone fight through the fire to find them hiding in the cellar?

"Hey!" Pete grasped Jupe's arm. "Hear that?"

There were sirens in the distance.

"It's about time!" said Bob.

"Hurry up, firemen!" pleaded Pete. "We haven't got all night!"

The sirens came closer and closer. Then there were more sirens, and still more. Then, one by one, the piercing mechanical wails stopped.

"Help!" cried Pete. "Help! Hey, you guys!"

The three waited. After what seemed an age, they heard a wrenching sound and a crash above them.

"I'll bet that's the window!" said Bob. "They're yanking the grille out of the window!"

Water thundered and gushed on the planks above them. Jupe felt wetness on his face, and on his shoulders and arms. Rivulets of dirty water spattered down all around him.

"We'll drown!" Pete yelled. "Stop! We're down here!"

The sound of rushing water ceased.

"Open the trap door!" Bob cried.

There was the protest of wood scraping on wood. The panel above them opened and a fireman looked down.

"They're here!" he shouted. "I found the kids!"

The fireman leaped into the cellar. An instant later Bob was being boosted up through the trap door to a second fireman, who seized him and sent him staggering toward the window. The iron grating was gone and two hose lines ran into the mail room. Bob scrambled over the sill and out onto the narrow walkway.

Bob had gone only a few steps when he heard Jupiter behind him. Pete followed, and the firemen who had pulled the boys from the cellar came after them. "Keep going!" ordered one of the men. "Move! Fast! The roof's going to cave in any second!"

The boys ran until they reached the open street. It was blocked with fire trucks. Hose lines lay in tangles from curb to curb.

"Thank heaven! You're safe!" Mr. Grear ran forward, clutching a paper sack of fried chicken.

"Hey you, get back!" shouted a fireman.

Mr. Grear retreated toward the crowd that had gathered across the street. The boys went with him. "They wouldn't let me go in after you," said Grear. "I told them you were in there, but they wouldn't let me go." He seemed to be in a daze.

"It's okay, Mr. Grear," said Jupiter. "We're safe." He took the sack of chicken from the old man and helped him sit down on a low wall in front of a little shopping center.

"Mr. Grear! Mr. Grear!" The boys looked around

to see Mr. Thomas hurrying toward them. He was dodging this way and that to get through the crowd of onlookers. "Mr. Grear, what happened? I saw the smoke. I was having dinner at a place near here and I saw the smoke. Mr. Grear, how did it start?"

Before Mr. Grear could comprehend that Thomas was questioning him, Beefy Tremayne came dashing around the corner onto Pacifica Avenue. His uncle trailed him, with Mrs. Paulson bringing up the rear.

"Mr. Grear!" cried Beefy. "You okay? Hey, are you boys all right?"

"We're okay," Pete assured him.

Beefy crouched beside Mr. Grear.

"I would have called you," said Grear, "but I was too concerned about the boys."

"We saw the smoke from our apartment and came running," said Beefy.

A shout went up across the street. Firemen scrambled to get clear of the adobe. Then the roof of the building fell in with a roar.

Flames leaped up against the sky. The thick walls of the old building still stood, but the firemen ignored them now. Hoses played steadily on the roofs and walls of buildings up and down the street.

Jupe looked at Mrs. Paulson and saw that she was crying.

"Please don't," said Beefy. "Please, Mrs. Paulson, it's only a building."

"Your father's publishing house!" sobbed Mrs. Paulson. "He was so proud of it!"

"I know," said Beefy, "but it *is* just a building. As long as no one was hurt . . ."

The young publisher stopped talking and looked at the boys in a questioning way.

"We were the last ones out," said Bob. "Nobody was hurt."

Beefy managed to smile. "That's what's important," he said to Mrs. Paulson. "And Amigos Press isn't wiped out—not by a long shot. Our inventory of books is safe in the warehouse and our plates are in storage. Why, we've even got the Bainbridge manuscript!"

"We have?" said Mrs. Paulson.

"Yes. I put it in my briefcase and took it home. So things aren't that bad, and . . ."

Beefy broke off. A man with a hand-held camera had stepped onto the street and was walking toward the fire.

"Uh-oh," said Beefy. "The television stations are covering this. I'd better find a phone."

"Why?" asked William Tremayne.

"I want to call Marvin Gray," Beefy explained, "to tell him the Bainbridge manuscript is safe. If he watches the news and finds out that Amigos Press burned down, he'll think the manuscript went with it unless I tell him differently."

Beefy headed for the filling station on the corner, where there was a pay telephone. At that moment, Jupiter became aware that there was a man approaching from across the street—a man whose face was ghastly white. He was bleeding badly from a wound on his scalp.

"Oh, gosh!" exclaimed Pete.

The blood coursed down the man's cheek and soaked the front of his shirt.

"What on earth?" said William Tremayne.

Jupiter started forward as the man collapsed in the street. A fireman ran to bend over the fallen man, and two policemen hurried to help him. Gingerly they turned him over on his back, and one of them looked quickly at the wound on his head.

"Say, I know him!" A stout woman pushed her way out of the crowd and went to the policemen. "He works in that film place there." She pointed toward Film Craft Laboratory, a solidly built brick building which was next to the ruins of Amigos Press. "I've seen him come and go lots of times," said the woman.

One of the policemen stood up. "I'll call an ambulance," he told his partner. "Then we'd better check out that film lab. Doesn't look as if this guy's going to be able to tell us anything. He might not wake up for quite a while!"

3

The Double Disaster

There was a brief account of the fire on the late news that night. Jupiter watched it with his aunt Mathilda and uncle Titus, with whom he lived. The next morning, he was up in time to see the *Los Angeles Now* show.

"Haven't you had enough of that fire?" said Aunt Mathilda as Jupe put the portable TV on the kitchen counter. "It could have killed you!"

Jupe sat down and began to sip his orange juice. "Maybe there'll be news about that man," he said.

"The one who collapsed in the street?" Aunt Mathilda sat down to watch, and Uncle Titus poured himself a second cup of coffee.

On the television screen, newscaster Fred Stone looked grave. "There was a double disaster in Santa Monica yesterday," he said. "Fire broke out in the historic Amigos Adobe on Pacifica Avenue at approximately six o'clock. The building, which housed the the offices of Amigos Press, was empty except for three young mail clerks. They were trapped by the flames, but were rescued unharmed by firemen."

The image of Stone faded from the television screen. It was replaced by scenes of the smoking ruins of Amigos Press. Stone's voice went on narrating. "The adobe building was completely destroyed. Damage is estimated at half a million dollars.

"As the fire burned, police discovered that a robbery had taken place at Film Craft Laboratory, immediately adjacent to the adobe. At some time between five and six, thieves entered the laboratory, which specializes in the restoration of old motion pictures. They made off with almost one hundred reels of film, the negatives of motion pictures made by actress Madeline Bainbridge more than thirty years ago. Miss Bainbridge, who was once a leading star, had just sold the motion pictures to Video Enterprises, which owns this station—Station KLMC—and its affiliates."

Stone appeared again on the screen. "There is a possible witness to the unusual robbery," he said. "Film technician John Hughes was working overtime at the laboratory. He was apparently beaten by the thieves in the course of the crime. He managed to make his way to the street, where he collapsed. Hughes regained consciousness briefly at Santa Monica Hospital this morning, and he is believed to have given a statement to detectives."

There were footsteps on the front porch and the doorbell chimed urgently. Jupe went to the door and admitted Pete and Bob.

"You watching the news?" said Pete. "I saw the early show. Whoever bopped that guy on the head yesterday also swiped a whole bunch of movies from that lab in Santa Monica!"

"And they were Madeline Bainbridge's movies," said Bob. "How's that for a coincidence?"

"Much too coincidental," declared Jupiter.

The boys followed Jupe to the kitchen. On the television, Fred Stone was reporting a late development in the Bainbridge case. "This morning, a telephone call was made to Charles Davie, president of Video Enterprises," he said. "Mr. Davie was told that the Bainbridge films would be returned to Video Enterprises upon payment of two hundred and fifty thousand dollars to the persons who are holding these films. Mr. Davie made no statement as to whether or not Video Enterprises would ransom the pictures, which are considered irreplaceable."

"What a gimmick!" exclaimed Pete. "Swiping old movies and holding them for ransom!"

Fred Stone went on with his newscast. "Following the robbery at the Santa Monica film laboratory last evening, Station KLMC was able to arrange an interview between Jefferson Long, veteran crime reporter for the station, and Marvin Gray, who has been Madeline Bainbridge's business manager for many years. We now bring you a broadcast of that taped interview."

Fred Stone turned to look at the television monitor to his left. A second later, Jupiter and his friends saw a sun-bronzed man with wavy white hair on the screen. He sat on a straight wooden chair in front of a fireplace and held a microphone. A clock on the mantel behind him showed the time as half past nine.

"Good evening, ladies and gentlemen," said the man. "This is Jefferson Long, your KLMC crime reporter, at the Bainbridge estate near Malibu.

"Tonight Marvin Gray, Madeline Bainbridge's longtime friend and confidant, has consented to talk with us about the films which were taken earlier this evening in the robbery of the Film Craft Laboratory. Perhaps Mr. Gray will also tell us something about Miss Bainbridge and her work, which many still remember."

The camera pulled back away from Jefferson Long, and the watchers saw Marvin Gray. He appeared grubby and insignificant next to the impressive Jefferson Long. He was smiling in a superior manner, however, as if Long amused him.

"I'm sure you remember Miss Bainbridge very well, Mr. Long," he said. "If I recall correctly, you were an actor once yourself. You had the role of Cotton Mather in Miss Bainbridge's last picture, *The Salem Story*. It was your first picture, wasn't it?"

"Well, yes," said Long, "but—"

"Also your last," said Marvin Gray.

"How unkind of him to put it that way," said Aunt Mathilda. "You'd think he didn't like Mr. Long."

"Perhaps he doesn't," said Jupiter.

Jefferson Long looked flustered, and he hurried into his interview. "I'm sure that Miss Bainbridge was very upset when she learned that her films had been stolen," he said. "We had hoped to see her in person."

"Miss Bainbridge doesn't see reporters, ever," said

Marvin Gray, "and she's resting this evening. Her doctor prescribed a sedative. As you say, she *is* upset."

"Of course," said Jefferson Long smoothly. "Mr. Gray, none of Miss Bainbridge's films have been seen by the public since she retired. What influenced her to sell them to television at this time?"

Marvin Gray smiled. "Thirty years ago, studio executives didn't realize that feature motion pictures would become valuable television attractions," he said. "Madeline Bainbridge did. She had a lot of faith in the future of television—although she doesn't care for the medium."

"She doesn't watch television?" asked Long.

"No, she doesn't. But thirty years ago, she knew how important it would be, and she purchased all the rights to the pictures she had made. She decided three weeks ago that the time was right. She signed an agreement with Video Enterprises, releasing the films to them. Video Enterprises took possession of the negatives this morning and had them moved to Film Craft Laboratory for inspection and repair."

"Then it's really KLMC's loss if the films aren't recovered," said Long.

"Yes, but it's a loss to the world, too. Miss Bainbridge is a great artist. She played memorable roles— Cleopatra, Joan of Arc, Catherine the Great of Russia, Helen of Troy. The portrayals will be lost forever if the films aren't recovered."

"Certainly that would be a calamity," said Long, "and all due to a crime that is unique in a city that has seen many bizarre crimes. I am sure we all wish for the prompt apprehension of the two men who broke into the laboratory, and for the speedy recovery of the stolen films."

The camera moved in close to Jefferson Long, who looked at his audience with great sincerity. "Ladies and gentlemen, this is Jefferson Long, coming to you on videotape from the estate where Madeline Bainbridge has lived for many years as a recluse, the beauty which helped make her a star hidden from all but a few close friends. Ladies and gentlemen, I thank you."

The screen went blank. Then Fred Stone was on camera again. "And now for other news . . ." he began.

Jupiter turned off the television. "It sounds like a publicity stunt, but it can't be that," he said. "That film technician was seriously hurt. And Marvin Gray overlooked a great opportunity to mention the Bainbridge memoirs. He would have mentioned them if he were looking for publicity."

Just then there was a crash on the front stoop.

"Oh, blast!" exclaimed an exasperated voice.

Jupiter went to the door. Beefy Tremayne was standing on the porch.

"I knocked over a flowerpot," said Beefy. "Sorry."

He stepped into the living room. "Jupe, I need help," he said. Jupe saw that there were circles under his eyes. "I need some private eyes. Worthington says you're good, and maybe you'll help me out. Uncle Will won't pay to hire a regular detective."

Pete and Bob had come in from the kitchen. They looked at Beefy with curiosity.

"What's the matter?" Jupiter asked.

"The Bainbridge memoirs," said Beefy. "The manuscript has disappeared. Somebody stole it!"

4

A Case of Witchcraft?

"Okay, I admit that I'm clumsy," said Beefy Tremayne. "I drop things and knock things over. However, I do pay attention to business, and I'm good at my business. I do not lose manuscripts!"

"Bushwa!" said William Tremayne.

Beefy had driven The Three Investigators from Rocky Beach to the high-rise building in West Los Angeles where he shared an apartment with his uncle. It was a modern security building; the garage doors were opened by a sonic device and the door from the lobby to the inner court was monitored by closed-circuit television. The boys had found William Tremayne lounging on a sofa in the living room of the apartment. He was smoking a long, slender cigar and staring at the ceiling in a disinterested way.

"I refuse to waste time and effort fussing about that

manuscript," he announced. "You've misplaced it in your usual blithering fashion, and it will show up. We don't need any aspiring juveniles to snoop around with magnifying glasses and fingerprint powder."

"We left our fingerprint powder at home today, Mr. Tremayne," said Jupe stiffly.

"I'm delighted to hear it," declared Tremayne. He continued to gaze at the ceiling. "Beefy, while you were out, the insurance adjustor was here. He asked a lot of idiot questions, and I didn't care for his tone. Just because I look after your financial interests, and just because the money from the insurance company will come to me for disbursement, there's no need for anyone to take the attitude that I had anything to gain from that fire."

"Uncle Will, they have to ask questions," said Beefy.

"You mean they have to make it look as if they're earning their money," snapped William Tremayne. "I only hope there's no delay in settling our claim. It's going to cost a fortune to relocate the offices and start operations again."

"I can start operating right now if I can just get my hands on that manuscript!" said Beefy.

"Then look for it!" said his uncle.

"I have looked. It isn't here!"

"Beefy, do you mind if we look?" asked Jupiter. "If you say it isn't here, I'm sure it isn't, but it won't hurt for us to double-check."

"Okay. Go ahead," said Beefy. He sat down and glared at his uncle while the boys searched the apartment. They looked behind every piece of furniture and into every cupboard and bookcase. There was no sign of a manuscript that could be the memoirs of an aging movie star.

"All right, Beefy, it isn't here," said Jupiter at last. "Now let's begin at the beginning. When did you last have the manuscript?"

Bob sat down near Beefy, took a small pad from his pocket, and prepared to take notes.

"Last night," said Beefy, "about nine-fifteen or nine-thirty. I'd taken the manuscript out of my briefcase and started to go through it. But after the fire, and seeing that man bleeding the way he was, I was too shook up to read. I felt as if I had to do something physical. So I put the manuscript down on the coffee table, and I changed into trunks and went down to the pool for a swim."

"Were you here?" Jupiter asked William Tremayne.

The older man shook his head. "I played bridge with friends last night. I didn't get home until nearly two."

"And when you got back from the pool, the manuscript was gone?" Jupe said to Beefy.

"Yes, it was. I noticed it the minute I came in."

"Could the apartment door have been left unlocked while you were in the pool?" Jupe asked. "Do you ever go down and leave the catch off?"

"Never," said Beefy. "And I'm sure it was locked last night, because I forgot my keys when I went down to the pool. The manager had to come up and let me in with his passkey."

Jupiter went to the apartment door, opened it, and

looked closely at the doorjamb and the lock. "There's no sign of forced entry. And the lobby door is always locked, isn't it? And this apartment is twelve stories above the street. Someone must have a set of keys."

Beefy shook his head. "There isn't a spare set, unless you count the master key that the manager has. And that's ridiculous. We've had the same manager for years. He wouldn't take a toothpick!"

Bob looked up from his notebook. "Your set and your uncle's set are the only ones?" he asked.

"Well, there was a set in my desk at work," said Beefy. "I kept them there in case I lost mine. But they would have been destroyed in the fire last night."

"Hm!" said Jupe. "So it would seem." He closed the apartment door and went to stand at the open window and look down at the pool, many stories below. "Someone came into this building, which is not easy to enter," he said. "Someone then got into this apartment, found the manuscript on the coffee table, picked it up, and took it away. How was that done?"

Pete came and stood beside Jupe. He didn't look down toward the pool. Instead he looked up toward the sky. "They flew in over the roof and came through the open window," he said, "in a very small helicopter. It's the only answer."

"How about a broomstick?" said Uncle Will sarcastically. "That would do nicely if someone wanted to come in through the window, and it narrows our field of suspects. The manuscript was taken by a witch."

Beefy started as if he had been struck. "A witch?"

he exclaimed. "That's . . . that's weird!"

"Why?" said his uncle. "Do you like the helicopter theory better?"

"It's just that it's strange that you mentioned a witch. I read some of the manuscript before I went down to the pool, and it had bits of really crazy gossip about Hollywood people. Bainbridge described a dinner party given by Alexander de Champley, the director. She said he was a magician and a black witch, and he wore the pentacle of Simon Magus!"

Beefy took a pen out of his pocket and began to sketch on the back of an envelope. "There was a drawing of the pentacle in the manuscript," he said. "A five-pointed star in a circle. Bainbridge said it was gold with a circle of rubies on the outside. Now, I've heard of Simon Magus. He was a wizard way back in the days of ancient Rome, and people believed that he could fly."

"Marvelous!" said Uncle Will. "This old friend of Madeline Bainbridge put on the pentacle of Simon Magus and flew in here and took the manuscript so that we wouldn't find out that he's an evil wizard."

"If anyone flew in, it wasn't Alexander de Champley," said Jupe. "He died more than ten years ago. But were there other scandalous stories in the memoirs?"

Beefy shook his head. "I don't know," he said. "I only read that one anecdote. It's certainly possible that Madeline Bainbridge knew the secrets of lots of prominent people."

"Then that could be it," said Jupiter. "That could be the reason the manuscript was taken. Some person she knows wants to prevent the publication of her story!"

"But how could that person know the manuscript was here?" asked Beefy.

"Easily!" Jupe began to pace back and forth. His eyebrows were drawn down in excited concentration. "Beefy, last night you called Marvin Gray after the fire and told him the manuscript was safe. Of course he told Madeline Bainbridge. Then Madeline Bainbridge called a friend—or perhaps Gray did—and that friend told a friend. Anyone could know."

"It wouldn't have been Bainbridge who told," said Beefy. "Marvin Gray says she doesn't use the telephone. But it's true that Gray might have passed the word on, without realizing what would happen. And Bainbridge's secretary still lives with her. Her name's Clara Adams. She might have done it."

"Of course," said Jupe. "Beefy, couldn't you arrange an interview with Miss Bainbridge? Then you could ask her whom she wrote about."

"She won't see me," said Beefy. "She doesn't see anyone at all. Marvin Gray took care of the negotiations on the contract."

"Then talk to Gray," urged Jupiter. "He must have read the manuscript."

Beefy groaned. "But I don't *want* to talk to Gray," he said. "He'll ask about the advance, and I don't want to give it to him until I've read the manuscript. And there was only one copy. If he finds out I don't have it, he'll have a stroke!"

"Then don't tell him," advised Jupe. "Tell him there might be some legal problems if you publish the manuscript, and that your lawyer has to look it over before the advance is paid. Ask him if Miss Bainbridge has proof of the stories in the manuscript. Ask him if she's still in touch with any of the people she knew, or if Clara Adams is in contact with anyone."

"I can't do it," said Beefy. "I'd blow it for sure. Gray would guess right away that something was up."

"Take Jupe with you," suggested Pete. "He's an expert at getting information from people, and they don't even know they've told him anything."

Beefy looked at Jupe. "Can you do that?" he asked.

"Usually I can," said Jupe.

"Very well." Beefy took an address book out of his pocket and headed for the telephone.

"You're not calling Marvin Gray?" said his uncle.

"I certainly am calling him," said Beefy, "and Jupe and I are going to see him this afternoon!"

5

The Haunted Grove

"Worthington tells me you boys operate as a team," said Beefy Tremayne. He and Jupiter were in his car, speeding north on the Coast Highway. "He says Bob is a good researcher, and Pete's the athlete of the group, and that you're a whiz at taking a few clues and figuring out what they mean. He also says that you're a mine of miscellaneous information."

"I enjoy reading," said Jupiter, "and fortunately I remember most of what I read."

"Lucky for you," said Beefy. "You couldn't have a handier talent."

The car slowed and turned off the highway onto a side road just outside the coastal community of Malibu. Beefy was silent as he drove up into the hills above the sea. After five minutes he braked again and left the curving mountain road for a narrow gravel road. He went on for a quarter of a mile, then pulled to a stop in front of a rustic gate. A sign over the gate indicated that they had reached the Half-moon Ranch.

"I don't know what I expected," said Beefy, "but it wasn't anything like this."

"It does look very ordinary," said Jupe. "You'd expect that a movie star who is also a recluse would live in a palatial mansion or at least have a ten-foot wall around her estate. There isn't even a lock on that gate."

Jupe got out of the car and held the gate open while Beefy drove through. Then Jupe got in and they headed up the driveway through a grove of lemon trees.

"It's strange that Gray didn't mention the sale of Bainbridge's films to you when he brought the manuscript in yesterday," said Jupiter.

"Very strange," Beefy agreed. "It will make a big difference in sales for the book."

"Was it Gray who chose you to be Bainbridge's publisher?" Jupe asked.

"I'm not sure," said Beefy. "He called me about six weeks ago and said that Bainbridge wanted to publish her memoirs. It's common knowledge that he handles all of her affairs, and he seemed to know what he was doing. I didn't ask him why he chose Amigos Press. I wonder if he's really as sharp as he appears to be. He should have let me know about the sale of the films."

The car emerged from the lemon grove, and a white frame ranch house came into view. It was large and plain, with a verandah that stretched across the front. Marvin Gray stood on the steps, squinting in the sunlight.

"Good afternoon," said Gray as Beefy clambered

out of the car. "I saw your dust as you came through the trees."

Gray frowned slightly at Jupe. "And who might this be?" he asked.

"My cousin, Jupiter Jones," said Beefy. His face flushed as he embarked on the cover story that he and Jupe had prepared. It was plain that he was not used to telling even small lies. "You saw him yesterday at Amigos Press," he went on. "He's learning the business. And he's taking a course in the history of motion pictures. I didn't think you'd mind if he came with me to see Madeline Bainbridge's home."

"I guess it's all right," said Gray. "But I'm surprised that you're here today, after the fire. I should think you'd have other things to attend to."

"If I weren't here, I'd be at home brooding about the fact that my office burned down," said Beefy.

Gray nodded. He turned and led the way up the steps. Then, instead of going into the house, he sat down in one of the wicker chairs on the porch. He motioned to his guests to take seats near him.

Beefy sat down. "Mr. Gray, I'm afraid there's going to be a delay in issuing the check for the advance on Miss Bainbridge's memoirs," he said. "I've looked through the manuscript and found several anecdotes which might cause legal problems. In one place, for example, there's the statement that a Hollywood director was a wizard. I know that the director is dead, but his heirs could sue. So I'm asking my attorney to look at the manuscript. In the meantime, Miss Bainbridge might give us the names of people who could back up her statements. And the addresses, of course."

"We certainly can't give you any addresses," said Marvin Gray. "Miss Bainbridge doesn't keep in touch with any of the old crowd."

"Well, perhaps you'd know how we could get in touch with some of the people," said Beefy. He was looking harassed and uncomfortable. "You've read through the manuscript, I'm sure, so . . ."

"No," said Marvin Gray, "I haven't read it. Miss Bainbridge gave it to me only yesterday afternoon. I couldn't help you anyway. I never was friends with any of those people. I was the chauffeur then, remember?"

"How about her secretary?" said Beefy hopefully.

"Clara Adams?" Gray looked surprised. "She hasn't left this property in years."

Beefy looked stumped, so Jupe came to his rescue. He looked around eagerly and asked, "Aren't we going to see Miss Bainbridge?" His voice was naive and somewhat brash.

"Miss Bainbridge doesn't see anyone but myself and Clara," said Marvin Gray. "Even if she was used to having visitors, she wouldn't want to see anyone today. She's upset about the theft of her films. She's upstairs resting, and Clara is with her, and I'd appreciate it if you kept your voice down."

"I'm sorry," said Jupe. He looked around curiously. "Miss Bainbridge is really a recluse, huh?" he said. "Doesn't anyone live here besides you and Clara Adams and Miss Bainbridge? Aren't there any servants?"

"We live very simply," said Gray. "Servants aren't necessary."

"I saw you on television this morning," said Jupe. "Is it true that Miss Bainbridge doesn't watch TV?"

"It's true," said Gray. "I watch, and I tell her about any news I think will interest her."

"It sounds kind of lonely," said Jupe. "Doesn't she see anybody at all? Don't you see anybody? I mean, don't you get tired of just being here all the time? And Clara Adams—doesn't she get tired of it?"

"I don't think so. I enjoy my own company pretty well, and Clara is completely devoted to Miss Bainbridge. I am, too, of course. Extremely devoted."

Jupiter turned to Beefy. "You see?" he said. "You don't have anything to worry about."

Gray looked at Beefy in a questioning way. "You were worried?" he said. "Why?"

"Well, Beefy said on the way up here he was kind of nervous," said Jupe. "He figured if anyone knew where Miss Bainbridge's manuscript was, they might try to swipe it the way they swiped her films, and hold it for ransom. If you told anyone where it is . . ."

"Now who would I tell?" said Gray.

"Sounds like you wouldn't tell anybody," said Jupe, "unless maybe somebody called. . . ."

"We have an unlisted number," said Gray. "People don't call. And we only use the telephone when it's absolutely necessary."

"Gosh, the kids at school aren't going to believe this," said Jupe. The stocky boy stood up. "May I wash my hands?" he asked.

"Of course." Gray pointed to the door. "Go straight back through the hall and past the stairs. There's a lavatory next to the kitchen."

"Thanks," said Jupe, and he went into the house.

The hall seemed dim after the sunlight on the porch. The living room on the left was sparsely furnished with straight-backed wooden chairs. The dining room on the right had a rude wooden table and backless benches. The wide staircase was uncarpeted. Jupe found the lavatory beyond it. He went in, closed the door, turned on the water, and opened the medicine cabinet above the sink. There was nothing there but a jar which had some dried leaves in it. They smelled like mint. Jupe closed the medicine cabinet, washed his hands, and then dried them on a towel that hung from a hook on the wall. The towel seemed to be homemade.

When Jupe left the lavatory, he looked into the kitchen—and blinked in amazement at the old-fashioned appliances there. The ancient refrigerator had exposed coils on top, and the old gas range did not even have pilot lights. The faucets over the sink were worn brass ones. Jupe guessed they had been installed when the house was first built many years before.

A row of glass jars was lined up on a counter near the sink. Jupe crossed to read the labels. He saw tansy and lupine, rose hips, mint leaves, and thyme. One jar puzzled him, for according to the label it contained deadly nightshade.

In a large jar at the very end of the row there were books of matches. Jupe looked at a few of them. They were all from various restaurants. Then he turned toward the window. A movement behind the house had caught his eye.

He found that he was looking out at a large grove

of live oaks. The trees were old and gnarled, with twisted trunks that branched out as they stretched above the second floor of the house. The dark green, spiny leaves shut out the sky and made the day seem gray. The oaks had been planted in wide-set rows, and among them two women were walking together. They wore gowns of some dark material, gowns that were caught in tightly at the waist, and which then flowed into wide skirts that brushed the ground. Both women had long hair, which they wore twisted into knots at the back of their heads. A sleek Doberman pinscher stalked behind them.

As Jupe stood watching, one of the women looked toward the house. Jupe gasped. He had seen pictures of Madeline Bainbridge in books about films, and it was Bainbridge he saw now under the old trees in that gray, dreary wood. Her blonde hair was now closer to white, but her lovely face was still remarkably youthful. After an instant she turned and walked on. Jupe didn't think she had noticed him.

Jupe took a step toward the window and found himself wishing for a glimpse of the sun. He felt chilled. There was an eerie sadness about the trees, and about the women who walked under the boughs dressed in dark, old-fashioned gowns.

A footstep sounded behind Jupe. "Finished washing your hands?" asked Marvin Gray.

Jupe jumped and almost cried out. Then he pointed toward the window. "Those trees make everything look so dark," he said.

"They do, don't they?" Gray agreed. "There's a rancher who used to live up the road who said the grove was haunted. It looks as if it might be, doesn't it? It was a cemetery once—a private one that belonged to the family that lived here. There were graves under the trees. They were moved when Miss Bainbridge bought the house, of course, but the woods still seem gloomy to me.

"I came to find you. Your cousin is ready to start back to town."

Jupe followed Gray back through the house. A few minutes later, he and Beefy were speeding away from Half-moon Ranch.

"Well, that visit was certainly a dead bust," complained Beefy. "We didn't get any leads on who could have stolen Bainbridge's manuscript."

"But we got plenty of food for thought," replied Jupiter.

"Such as?"

"Gray lied to us about one thing. Madeline Bainbridge wasn't upstairs. She was outside with another woman—Clara Adams, I suppose. Gray may tell lots of lies. There are matchbooks from restaurants out in the kitchen. He may get around more than he pretends."

"But why would he lie?" asked Beefy.

"To protect Madeline Bainbridge," said Jupe. "She isn't any ordinary recluse. She's a very odd lady. She and Clara Adams were wearing old-fashioned black gowns—they looked like Pilgrim ladies. And there's a jar in the kitchen that's filled with deadly nightshade."

"You're kidding!" exclaimed Beefy. "Deadly nightshade is a poison!"

"I know," Jupe said. "Madeline Bainbridge may be

one of the most fascinating characters I've come across. A lady who has changed very little in thirty years. I recognized her immediately. A lady who keeps poison in her kitchen, who goes around dressed like a Pilgrim, and who owns an oak grove that was once a cemetery. According to Gray, it's supposed to be haunted. At least, that's what some people say. And from the looks of it, it wouldn't surprise me if that were true!"

6

The Magic Circle

"You don't find nightshade in the ordinary kitchen!" said Jupiter Jones. He was sitting behind the desk in The Three Investigators' headquarters, an ancient mobile home trailer that was hidden away behind heaps of artfully arranged junk in a far corner of The Jones Salvage Yard. Pete and Bob had returned from the library, where Jupe had sent them to do some research while he was out with Beefy. Jupe had just finished telling them of his visit to the Bainbridge ranch.

"Nightshade is a name for a whole family of plants," Jupe went on. "Many of them are narcotic poisons, and some of them were once used in magic rituals."

"Madeline Bainbridge must be a real weirdo," said Pete. "Poison in her kitchen and a private cemetery out in the back!"

"It isn't a cemetery now," Jupe pointed out. "It *used* to be one. But there *was* something eerie and unreal

43

about the place. It gave me the creeps."

"A cemetery and strange herbs," said Bob thought-
fully. He took his notebook out of his pocket. "It fits.
It fits beautifully!"

Bob began to flip through his notes. "I looked up
magic and witchcraft because Bainbridge had that
story about the director Alexander de Champley being
a wizard. It must have been important to her, or she
wouldn't have taken time to draw the pentacle of
Simon Magus in the manuscript.

"Now there are several different kinds of witches.
There's the Halloween kind, who is sort of a comic-
strip hag with warts on her chin. Then there are the
evil ones, the sorcerers and witches who can do dread-
ful things because they worship the devil. He helps
them out, according to the superstitious, and I guess
there's no limit to what you can do if Satan is backing
you."

Pete scowled. "I don't believe a word of it," he said,
"but would you hurry up? I don't like hearing about
stuff like that."

"Okay, then you'll like the rest better," said Bob.
"There's a form of witchcraft called the Old Religion.
People who practice it say that it goes back to very
ancient times. It's a sort of fertility cult—it has a lot
to do with growing things and harvests. It's kind of
nice, really. The witches believe that they have the
power to make things happen because they're in tune
with the power of the universe. They're organized
into groups called covens, and each coven has thirteen
people in it. They meet at special places, like a cross-
roads. An even better place is—guess where?"

"A . . . a cemetery?" said Jupe after a second.

"Right!" said Bob. "When they meet they have regular rites. They eat freshly gathered food and they worship Selena, or Diana, the moon goddess. They perform their rites at night, not because they're wicked, but just so the neighbors won't see them and gossip. The rituals can be performed at any time, but there are four main feasts, called Sabbats, every year. An Old Religion witch always attends the Sabbats. These happen on April thirtieth, August first, October thirty-first—which is our Halloween, of course—and the second eve of February."

Bob closed his notebook. "That's all I got today. There's more, and we can take some of the books out of the library if we need to. I just wonder, if someone wanted the Bainbridge manuscript suppressed, could it be because that person was a witch? It could be someone in the film colony who either was a member of the Old Religion and didn't want it known, or perhaps someone who was a Satanist."

Pete shivered. "If we do have a witch mixed up in this, I hope it's one of the Old Religion witches," he said. "I don't think I want to mess with anybody who worships the devil."

Jupiter nodded. "A Satanist could be a person who is completely without a conscience," he said. "Or he could be a person who is somewhat simple-minded. In either case, he could be dangerous. But what did you do, Pete, while Bob was reading about witches?"

"I was reading about Madeline Bainbridge," said Pete. "I went back into the microfilm files."

The Second Investigator took an untidy sheaf of

papers out of his pocket and began to read his penciled notes.

"She came here from Fort Wayne, Indiana, when she was eighteen. She'd won a beauty contest and the prize was a trip to Hollywood. Alexander de Champley spotted her while she was touring the FilmArt Studio. Three weeks later she had a contract with FilmArt and was set to play Mary Queen of Scots in Champley's version of the picture. That's some kind of an all-time record for getting discovered and cast in a picture."

Pete looked up at his friends. "All the stories said she was very, very beautiful."

"She's still beautiful," said Jupe. "I saw her today. Anything more, Pete?"

"Just general stuff," said Pete. "She seems to have been a pretty quiet person. She didn't get into scandals. She made a lot of very good pictures. Most of her roles were historical, like Cleopatra and Catherine the Great. She had the best leading men, but she never bothered with them much once a picture was finished. She didn't make lots and lots of friends. She was sort of a loner, and there was never any gossip to link her romantically with any actor until the last of her leading men—Ramon Desparto."

"What about him?" asked Bob.

"He died shortly after he finished making the picture *The Salem Story*. That was a very strange picture about the witch trials in Salem and—"

"And there we have witchcraft again," interrupted Jupe.

"Right. But this movie was very hokey. The plot was weird. Bainbridge played a Puritan maiden who is accused of witchcraft, and who saves herself by running away with an Indian brave so that she doesn't get hanged. Ramon Desparto played the Indian brave, and he also got engaged to Madeline Bainbridge just before shooting started on the picture. There was some nasty talk that the engagement was just to help his career. He got engaged a lot to his leading ladies. Not long after *The Salem Story* was finished, he was killed in an auto accident. It happened after a party at Bainbridge's ranch, and Bainbridge had some kind of nervous collapse. She never worked again. She bought up all of her pictures and spent the next thirty years keeping out of sight."

"And avoiding her old friends?" said Jupiter.

"There may not have been that many old friends," said Pete. He unfolded a photocopy of a picture that he had tucked in with his notes and handed it across the desk to Jupe. "This picture was taken at the Academy Awards dinner the year *The Salem Story* was made," he said. "That group of people is called 'Madeline Bainbridge's magic circle' because they're the ones she spent her time with. There aren't so many. Marvin Gray isn't in the picture, though."

"He wasn't a friend then," Jupiter reminded Pete. "He was still just the chauffeur."

Jupe studied the picture and read the caption. Madeline Bainbridge and the darkly handsome Ramon Desparto sat at the head of the table. On the star's other side was Jefferson Long, looking very young and handsome. The caption identified a man named Elliott Farber as Bainbridge's favorite cameraman. An actor named Charles Goodfellow sat next to an actress named Estelle DuBarry. Nicholas Fowler, a script-writer, was there, and so was Clara Adams, who sat next to character actor Ted Finley. Janet Pierce was identified as costume designer for the Salem picture, and Lurine Hazel and Marie Alexander were actresses. A very plain girl named Gloria Gibbs stared straight ahead, and was referred to as Desparto's secretary.

"How interesting!" said Jupiter Jones. "A magic circle indeed! There are thirteen people here, and thirteen at a table is considered unlucky—unless you are a witch. For a coven, thirteen is the right number!"

Jupe beamed at his fellow investigators. "Bob, your notes indicate that August first is one of the four great Sabbats of the year. This happens to be the first of August. Was Madeline Bainbridge a witch? Is she still a witch? If so, who is in her coven today? There's one way to find out! Who's game for a ride up the coast to the Malibu hills tonight?"

"Hey, that's nuts!" cried Pete. Then he grinned. "What time do we start?"

7

The Creature in the Dark

It was dusk when The Three Investigators reached the spot where the narrow gravel road to Bainbridge's ranch crossed the paved mountain road that wound up through the Malibu hills. Jupe stopped, resting on the seat of his bike. Pete and Bob drew level with him, and Jupe pointed to the left.

"The Bainbridge place is down that way," he said. "I've gone over a map of this area. There are several places where a coven could meet, if Bainbridge is going to pay attention to the rules. One is this cross-roads right here. One is the grove of trees behind her house—the place that was once a cemetery. And one is about half a mile north of her house, where two footpaths meet. I suggest we spread out to make sure we don't miss Bainbridge if she leaves her property."

Jupe dug into a knapsack that was strapped to the handlebars of his bicycle. "There's a dog, so we've got

49

to be careful," he warned. "We can't get too close to the house. I brought the walkie-talkies."

He produced three small radio sets which he himself had rigged up in his workshop at the salvage yard. Each set was a little larger than a regular transistor radio, and consisted of a combined speaker and microphone. There were also three belts with copper wire sewn to them, and each had a lead-in wire which could be plugged into a radio. The belt with the wire acted as an antenna, and the little radios operated like CB radios, broadcasting for about half a mile. When the user wanted to speak into the microphone, he pressed a button on the side of the radio set. When he wanted to listen, he released the button.

Jupe handed a radio set to Bob, and one to Pete. "I'll watch from the hill behind that haunted-looking grove," he said. "Bob, you can hide in among the lemon trees between the road and the house. Pete, your post can be on the north side of the house—that's the left side. There's a field there with some tall grass that you can use for cover. If Madeline Bainbridge leaves the house tonight, we'll spot her no matter which way she goes. Keep an eye out for cars, and for other people walking around. They might lead us to a Sabbat."

The other two boys murmured in agreement and took the radios. The three then rode down the gravel road to the front gate of the Bainbridge ranch. There they hid their bikes in the tall weeds beside the road, and separated. Bob's slim figure disappeared among the lemon trees. Pete went on down the gravel road toward the north side of the property. Jupe trudged up through the fields, skirting the house and the grove of live oaks. On the hillside behind the grove he found a clump of manzanita. He crouched behind the shrub and held his walkie-talkie to his mouth.

"This is One," he said softly. "Come in, Two."

He released the button on the radio and listened. "This is Two," said Pete's voice. "I'm in the field to the north of the house. I see lights in the house, at the back, and I see people moving around inside, but I can't tell what they're doing. Over."

"Stay put," ordered Jupiter. "How about you, Three?"

"I can see the front of the house from the lemon grove," said Bob. "It's all dark. Over."

"Now we wait," said Jupiter. "Over and out."

He leaned back against the hillside and studied the grove of oaks, which completely hid the ranch house from view. The trees looked even more sinister by moonlight than they had that afternoon. The moon was climbing into the sky now, casting intense black shadows under the gnarled limbs.

The radio in Jupe's hand crackled.

"This is Two," said Pete. "The lights in the house have just gone out. Now there are some little lights out in back. Over."

A tiny light flickered in the dark woods below. Then Jupe saw a second light. Then a third.

Jupe pressed the button on his radio. "They're moving into the live-oak grove," he said softly. "I can see candles."

He waited. The candle lights moved beneath the twisted trees. Then the movement stopped and the candles glowed steadily. And there were more lights.

"I'm going in closer," said Jupe into the walkie-talkie. "You stay where you are for the moment."

He released the button on the radio and slipped out from behind the manzanita. He half-slid down the hillside until he reached level ground behind the Bainbridge house. Then, like a chubby shadow, he stole from bush to bush until he was at the edge of the stand of oak trees. He paused, looking toward the candle flames that burned inside the grove. There were dozens of lights now, forming a circle, and for a moment Jupe could see only the candles against the darkness that pressed in around them. Then, beyond the candles appeared a woman who stared straight ahead into the night. It was Madeline Bainbridge. Her long, white-blonde hair was loose on her shoulders, and she wore a wreath of flowers on her head. She moved slowly forward into the circle of light.

There was a movement beyond Madeline Bainbridge. A second woman appeared out of the darkness. She carried a tray that was heaped high with fruit. It was the woman Jupe had seen with Madeline Bainbridge that afternoon. Jupe knew she must be Clara Adams. She entered the circle of light and put the tray down on a table draped with a black cloth.

Another face glimmered in the dark wood. It was Marvin Gray. He, too, wore a wreath of flowers on his dark hair. Jupe realized that he could scarcely see Gray's body. The man wore a black robe. So did the two women. They were invisible in the night except for their faces and for the circlets of flowers that crowned their heads.

"I will draw the circle," intoned Marvin Gray. His hands moved, white against his black robe. The blade of a knife glinted in the candlelight.

Jupe backed away from the ghostly woods and the strange trio under the branches. When he felt it was safe to speak, he pressed the button on his walkie-talkie. "Pete? Bob? I'm in the field just behind the grove. I'm pretty sure there's a Sabbat going on here."

"Be right there," said Bob.

"Me, too," Pete said.

Pete appeared in a very few minutes, coming as quietly as a ghost. Then Bob came stealing toward them through the night.

"There are only three people, but they're getting ready for some sort of ceremony," Jupe told his friends. "Marvin Gray has a knife."

"I read about that today," said Bob. "He'll draw a circle on the ground with the knife. Witches believe that the circle increases their power."

"Let's watch," said Jupiter.

Bob and Pete silently followed Jupe in among the trees, looking nervously ahead. What strange rites were they about to witness? They saw the three white-faced people standing in the ring of candlelight. They saw Madeline Bainbridge lift a cup high and close her eyes as if she were praying. The boys held their breath.

Then, suddenly, Pete uttered a small, wordless cry of terror. For out of the darkness, some silent-footed beast had come to stand beside him. For an instant the creature was still. Pete could feel its hot breath on him. Then it growled, low and ominously.

8

Murder by Magic?

"What's that?" cried Marvin Gray. "Who's there?"

The three boys froze, and the growling went on and on.

Clara Adams put her hands to her mouth and gazed out from the circle of light. Madeline Bainbridge did not move. She was like a carving in ivory and ebony. From somewhere beneath his black robe, Marvin Gray pulled out a flashlight. He charged toward The Three Investigators and the flashlight snapped on. Jupe saw that the animal standing near Pete was a dog—the sleek Doberman he had seen that afternoon. Obviously the animal had been trained to hold intruders motionless, but not to attack unless greatly provoked; it made no move to harm Pete.

"What do you boys think you're doing here?" demanded Gray.

Jupe felt Gray's gaze on him and his heart sank.

How could he explain to this man that Beefy Tremayne's young cousin, who had been such a polite visitor that afternoon, had returned after dark to spy on Gray and the two women?

"Who's there, Marvin?" called Madeline Bainbridge.

"Bunch of kids. They probably came up from Malibu," said Gray. "Ought to call the sheriff and have them thrown in the clink!"

Jupe's heart began to beat wildly. Was it possible that Gray didn't recognize him?

"Hey, mister," said Jupe. "Call the dog, huh?"

"All right, Bruno," said Gray. "Here, boy!"

The dog stopped growling and went to Gray.

"Now what are you doing here?" asked Gray again. "Can't you see this is private property?"

"Not in the dark," said Jupe boldly. "We were hiking in the hills. We got off the path and we couldn't find our way back."

"Marvin!" Madeline Bainbridge sounded impatient. "Let the boys go, and come back. You're holding us up!"

Jupiter looked past Gray to Madeline Bainbridge. Then he glanced at Gray. Gray looked hesitant. He obviously couldn't decide what to do.

Jupe started toward Bainbridge. "We're really very sorry," he said. "We didn't mean to disturb you."

"The circle!" gasped Clara Adams. "He's profaning the circle!"

Jupe went on toward the table where the women stood, repeating his apologies. One hand was at his belt, unfastening the antenna of the walkie-talkie.

With the other hand he held the little radio set at his side, out of sight of the women. He was quite near the table when the antenna came away from his waist. He stumbled on something in his path and fell, stretched out full length on the ground, his head and shoulders almost under the table.

"Marvin!" cried Madeline Bainbridge.

Jupe's hands disappeared for a moment under the black cloth that draped the table. Then he pulled himself to his hands and knees. "Sorry," he said again. "That was clumsy of me. We didn't mean to upset you, honest. If you could just point us in the direction of the road . . ." Jupe got to his feet.

"Marvin, show these boys how to get to the main road," said Madeline Bainbridge.

"Thank you," said Jupiter.

Gray led The Three Investigators out from under the trees. He pointed across the fields to the place where, as the boys knew, the paved road led down to the Coast Highway. "There!" said Gray. "Keep going until you hit the road. Then turn right and don't come back."

"Thanks a lot, mister," said Pete.

Gray stood watching as The Three Investigators walked away through the tall, moonlit grass.

"He isn't going to take his eyes off us until we're off this property," predicted Bob.

"I don't blame him," said Jupiter. "Would *you* want strangers at secret rites in your backyard? Let's hope that he doesn't look under the table and discover that I put my walkie-talkie there!"

"So that's why you fell!" exclaimed Pete.

"I thought it might be interesting to listen in on any conversation that occurs after we leave," said Jupe. "I wrapped part of the antenna wire around the set so that the button is pressed down. The radio won't receive, but it should send. Let's not go too far or we'll be out of range."

The boys stepped from the meadow onto the paved road. Bob looked back. Marvin Gray had disappeared. "He's probably back in the grove of oak trees," Bob said. He followed Jupe and Pete down the road to the shelter of a clump of bushes.

"Turn on your set, Bob," said Jupiter. "Let's listen in on the coven."

Bob knelt beside the bushes and turned the knob that activated his set.

". . . gone for the time being," they heard Gray say. "They won't try to come back. Not after Bruno pinned them down that way."

"I had hoped that Bruno was locked up someplace," Jupe muttered.

Gray was speaking again. "It was dumb to let them go," he declared.

"What should we have done?" said Madeline Bainbridge.

"Run them off a cliff!" growled Gray.

"Marvin!" cried a woman's voice. It was not Madeline Bainbridge, so the boys assumed that Clara Adams had been shocked at Gray's suggestion.

"Well, I don't like kids snooping around," said Gray. "They'll go home and talk about what they've seen. Next thing we know, there'll be photographers and reporters hiding behind every tree. I can see the headlines now: 'Mystery Rites at Movie Star's Ranch!' Before you know it, the cops are poking around and—"

"We hardly need to worry about the police," said Madeline Bainbridge. "We're doing nothing wrong."

"Not now!" said Gray.

"Not ever!" said the actress.

"Then you *want* the cops up here?" asked Gray. "You should have used your power on those kids, just the way you did on Desparto that night!"

"I never harmed Ramon!" cried the movie star. "Not even when he betrayed me!"

"Of course not!" Gray's voice was mocking. "You wished him long life and happiness."

"Marvin, don't!" Clara Adams pleaded.

"You keep bringing that up!" The actress's voice was rough with anger. "Over and over again. All right, I was furious with Ramon. But I didn't hurt him. I wouldn't use my power to hurt anyone, and you know it. In fact, you're counting on it, aren't you?"

"Madeline! Please!" said Clara Adams.

"Okay, okay!" grumbled Gray. "There's no use going on with the rite now. Let's get into the house." He raised his voice. "Bruno! Here, Bruno!"

"Perhaps we should leave the dog outside," said Clara Adams, "just in case those boys come back."

"They won't come back," predicted Gray. "And if we leave him out, he'll get restless at three in the morning and set up a howl, and I'll have to get up to let him in. That's what we get for raising a guard dog who thinks he's a member of the family."

There was no more conversation from the walkie-talkie. After a few moments, Jupiter drew a deep breath. "Marvin Gray wanted Madeline Bainbridge to use her power on us, just as she used it on Ramon Desparto," he said. "What, I wonder, did she do to Desparto?"

"Nothing, according to her," answered Bob. "She said she never harmed anybody."

"Desparto died in an auto accident," said Pete. "The brakes on his car failed when he was leaving here one night after a party."

"Was it a party?" said Jupiter. "Or was it like the ritual we saw tonight? One thing we now know for sure: Madeline Bainbridge *is* a witch, or she thinks she's a witch. And she believes she has some kind of power."

"The power to . . . to kill someone?" said Pete. His voice was very low.

"Murder by magic?" Bob shook his head. "Impossible!"

"Perhaps," said Jupiter. "However, it appears that Madeline Bainbridge feels some guilt about Desparto. She wouldn't deny her responsibility so furiously if she didn't believe it was possible for her to have hurt him in some fashion."

"That Marvin Gray," said Pete. "Why'd he get her all stirred up that way? He didn't have to rake up that stuff from the past."

"Perhaps he's manipulating her," said Jupe. "He may be the real power in her household—perhaps the only power."

"I don't like him," said Pete.

"Nor do I," agreed Jupe. "Not after hearing him over the walkie-talkie. The man's a bully. I wonder if he tells lies just to protect Madeline Bainbridge's privacy. He may be even more interested in protecting his own."

"Jupe?" said Bob. "Could Gray have been involved in the theft of her manuscript?"

Jupe shrugged. "I don't see why or how. He couldn't have taken the manuscript himself—he was being interviewed by Jefferson Long when it was stolen. And he has no apparent motive for theft. Quite the opposite. As Bainbridge's business manager, it's to his advantage to have the book published and earning money. But did he talk to someone—anyone—about the book? Or did Bainbridge? After what we've heard tonight, I'm almost sure the answer to the mystery of the missing manuscript is hidden in Bainbridge's past —in that magic circle which existed long ago."

Jupe stood up. "We've done all we can do tonight. I'll go and retrieve my walkie-talkie and meet you where we left our bikes. Tomorrow . . . tomorrow we investigate the former coven."

"If that's what it was," said Bob.

"I think that's just what it was," said Jupiter, and he started across the fields toward the haunted wood.

9

The Crime Fighter

"You're kidding!" said Beefy Tremayne. "Madeline Bainbridge really is a witch?"

Beefy was guiding his sports car along Santa Monica Boulevard. Jupiter sat beside him, and Pete and Bob were squeezed into the back seat.

"She's a witch now," declared Jupiter, "and it seems more than likely that she was a witch back in the days when she was active in films. We think that she may have headed a coven, and that sinister things may have gone on among the people in it. Someone who was involved may well want to prevent her memoirs from being published. We plan to interview her close associates to see if we can establish some connection with Bainbridge within the last couple of days. We have to find someone who knew where the manuscript was night before last."

"But you can't expect anyone to admit he knew

61

where the manuscript was," objected the young publisher. "I mean, if that person stole it."

"We don't intend to ask about the manuscript at all," answered Jupe, "at least in the beginning. First we have to find out who in the coven is still in touch with Madeline Bainbridge, or is getting news of her. I don't think anyone will be afraid to admit a connection with her."

Beefy turned north on La Brea Avenue toward Hollywood.

"And you're going to talk to Jefferson Long for openers?" he said. "Long, the crime fighter? He's so foursquare and true-blue. I just can't imagine him being mixed up in anything weird like a coven."

"He wasn't always Jefferson Long, the crime fighter," Jupe pointed out. "He used to be an actor, and he was in Bainbridge's last picture. He had to know Ramon Desparto. Also, it's logical to begin our interviews with him, since we know where to find him. The offices of Video Enterprises, which include the studios for Station KLMC, are on Fountain Street just off Hollywood Boulevard. I called there earlier this morning, and he agreed to see me."

"Did you tell him why you wanted to talk with him?" asked Beefy.

"Not exactly. I said I was doing a report for my school paper as a summer project."

"Long must like publicity," said Pete from the back seat. "Even publicity in a school paper."

"Perhaps we all would, if we were in the public eye," said Jupiter. He glanced at Beefy. "It's really nice of you to drive us," he said. "We could have taken the bus."

"If I stayed at home, I'd only stew and worry," declared Beefy. "I'm kind of lost without an office to go to. Besides, you guys fascinate me. I don't think I'd dare just walk in on somebody like Jefferson Long."

Bob laughed. "Jupe doesn't scare easily."

"And how are you going to find the other people in the magic circle?" asked Beefy.

Pete answered, "My father works for a movie studio. He's getting us the addresses of Madeline Bainbridge's friends through the unions."

Beefy had been navigating carefully down Hollywood Boulevard. Now he turned right onto Fountain and pulled to the curb in front of a building that looked like a huge cube of dark glass. "We'll park here and wait," he said as Jupe got out. "Take your time."

"Right," said Jupe. He turned and went into the building.

The reception room was cool, shielded from the glare outside by polarized glass. The tanned young woman at the desk directed Jupe to the elevator, and he rode up to the fourth floor.

Jefferson Long's office was filled with glass and chrome and furniture upholstered in black leather. The windows faced north, toward the Hollywood Hills. Long sat behind a teakwood desk, his back to the view, and smiled at Jupiter.

"Nice to see you," said the crime reporter. "I'm always glad to do what I can to help young people."

Jupiter had a feeling that Long had made that short speech hundreds of times before.

"Thank you very much," said Jupiter in his most humble voice. He gazed at Long, and he let his round, cheerful face take on a look of almost idiotic innocence. "I saw your telecast the other morning," he said. "The interview you did at Madeline Bainbridge's estate. I was surprised! I didn't know that you were an actor and that you knew Madeline Bainbridge."

Jefferson Long's smile vanished suddenly. "I have done more important things in my life than being an actor and knowing Madeline Bainbridge," he said. He swung around in his chair and gestured toward the shelves that lined one side of his office. "The law enforcement people would be the first to agree."

Jupiter got up and went to the shelves. There he saw plaques and medallions from cities up and down the coast. There were photographs of Long with the police chiefs of various large and small towns in California, Nevada, and Arizona. There was also a framed parchment announcing that Jefferson Long was an honorary member of a sheriff's posse.

"Wow!" said Jupe. He hoped that he sounded properly impressed.

"I have some scrapbooks, too," declared Long. "You can look through them if you're interested."

"That would be super!" said Jupiter eagerly. "And a friend told me you're doing a series on drug abuse. That must be pretty exciting."

Jefferson Long's handsome face flushed. "It is. Can you imagine, even some people who are employed in legitimate pharmaceutical firms are involved in the illicit distribution of drugs? But I won't be able to put my series together this year. Some people not very far from here believe that it's more important to spend money on moldy old movies than on producing a documentary series on a major problem like drug abuse."

"Oh," said Jupiter. "Oh, well. I see. That's too bad, I guess. But the Madeline Bainbridge movies must have been very expensive."

"They will be even more expensive when they have been ransomed," said Long.

"That's tough luck for you, I guess," said Jupiter. "Except maybe it could be a break, couldn't it? I mean, you're in one of the movies!"

"*The Salem Story* was an extremely bad movie," said Jefferson Long. "In fact, it was such a flop that after the premiere, I never got another job as an actor. I found a much more satisfying career as a crime reporter."

"But Madeline Bainbridge retired," said Jupe. He was rambling like an artless youngster. "My aunt Mathilda remembers Madeline Bainbridge, and she says there was always some mystery about her. She said people used to say strange things about her and her friends. They used to talk about Madeline Bainbridge's coven."

"Coven?" Jefferson Long's face was suddenly wary, as if he sensed some enemy. He smiled stiffly. "Ridiculous," he said. "A coven is a group of witches."

"Yes," said Jupiter. "You worked with Miss Bainbridge. Was there a coven?"

"Certainly not!" declared Jefferson Long. "That is, so far as I know, there was no coven. Madeline Bainbridge's friends were—they were just the people she worked with, that's all."

"Did you know them?" Jupiter asked.

"Well, certainly. I was one of them."

"Well, maybe some of them knew something you didn't know," said Jupe. He gazed at Long without blinking. "Do you keep in touch with any of the others? Do you know where I could reach them? Or maybe you'd be able to put me in touch with Madeline Bainbridge herself."

"Certainly not!" exclaimed Long. "I don't have anything to do with those people any more. My friends are all in law enforcement. As for Bainbridge, I haven't seen her for thirty years—and I don't care if I don't see her for another thirty! She was a spoiled, temperamental would-be actress. Almost as bad as that Desparto character she was engaged to. Now there was a real ham!"

"He died after a party at her house, didn't he?"

"Yes." Jefferson Long looked old then, and his eyes were bleak. "After a party. Yes."

He straightened up and shook himself, as if shaking off a bad memory. "But that . . . that was a long time ago," he said. "I never think about those days now. No use dwelling in the past. And why are we talking so much about Madeline Bainbridge, anyway? I assume you've come because you're interested in my crime-fighting programs."

"I came because of Madeline Bainbridge," said Jupe simply. "I'm doing a paper on her for my course in the history of films. If the paper's good enough, it'll get published in the school journal."

Jefferson Long looked intensely annoyed. "I wish you good luck," he said coldly. "Now you'll have to excuse me. I can't give you any more time. I have a luncheon appointment."

"I understand," said Jupe. He thanked Long and left.

"Well?" said Beefy as Jupe got into the car.

"Jefferson Long does not like Madeline Bainbridge, and he doesn't like the idea of her films being shown on television," Jupe reported. "Video Enterprises isn't going to finance a series he wants to do on drug abuse because they spent so much money on the Bainbridge pictures. Long says he hasn't seen Bainbridge for thirty years and he hasn't kept up with any of her friends. Also, he denies that there was a coven. He may be telling the truth about everything else, but I think he was lying about the coven. Actually, I think that there is something odd about Jefferson Long, but I can't quite say what it is."

Pete chuckled in the back seat. "You'll figure it out. You always do," he said. "Anyway, here's something else to work on. I called my father at the studio while you were gone. He's got an address for us already. Elliott Farber was Bainbridge's favorite cameraman, and he was in the magic circle at that Academy Awards dinner. He isn't a cameraman any longer. He runs a television repair shop on Melrose. Let's go over there!"

10

The Witch's Curse

It was not necessary for The Three Investigators to fabricate a story about a school journal in order to see Elliott Farber. The former cameraman was not protected by a receptionist, and the three boys had only to walk into his dusty little shop in order to talk with him. Once they were in the shop—a narrow hole-in-the-wall sandwiched between a barber shop and an upholsterer—Jupe said, quite simply, "Mr. Farber, you were Madeline Bainbridge's favorite cameraman, weren't you?"

Elliott Farber was a thin man with a yellowish tint to his skin. He squinted at the boys through the smoke that wafted from the cigarette between his lips. "Don't tell me," he said. "Let me guess. You're old movie buffs."

"Something like that," said Jupe.

Farber smiled and leaned back against a counter.

"I worked with Bainbridge on almost every picture she ever made," he said. "She was tremendous. Great actress!"

Farber dropped his cigarette to the floor and ground it out with his foot. "She was beautiful, too. Some of the so-called glamour queens needed every bit of makeup and every trick of lighting to look good. They had to have every break the cameraman could give them. That's why I quit the business. I got sick of taking the blame if some dame didn't look enough like Cleopatra, Queen of the Nile. But with Bainbridge, there was no sweat. She was purely and simply beautiful. I couldn't make a mistake when I was filming one of her scenes."

"Was she difficult to work with?" asked Jupe.

"Oh, she liked to get her own way, once she got established. That's how we all got involved in that horrible turkey about witches and Puritans."

"*The Salem Story?*" prompted Jupe.

"Right," said Farber. "Ramon Desparto thought that one would be great. Madeline was nuts about him, so anything he wanted, he got. Madeline saw to it. We used to worry about her—that he'd wreck her career."

"That's what he did, didn't he?" asked Pete, who had been listening quietly. "I mean, after he died, she was so heartbroken she didn't work again."

"She blamed herself," said Farber. "She and Desparto had quarreled just before he had the auto accident that killed him. She'd said some pretty nasty things to him. Not that I blame her. He was playing around with another actress, Estelle DuBarry, and Madeline was jealous. If you're organizing some fan club for Madeline, or doing an article for some kid magazine, you could just forget I told you that bit. No sense in stirring up old troubles."

"Do you ever see Madeline Bainbridge these days, Mr. Farber? Or talk with her?" asked Jupiter.

"Nope. Nobody sees her. Nobody's in touch with her at all."

Bob showed Mr. Farber the copy of the picture he had found at the library. "Wasn't Estelle DuBarry one of the people who were very close to Madeline Bainbridge?" he asked. "She's in this photo that was taken at an awards dinner."

"Oh, that?" Farber took the picture from Bob. "Yes. The magic circle. There they are—all thirteen of them —including yours truly."

"Isn't thirteen an odd number to have at a dinner table?" said Jupe.

Farber smiled. "Not if you're a witch," he said.

"Then there *was* a coven!" cried Bob.

Now Farber laughed out loud. "Sure. Why not? Madeline was a witch—or at least she thought she was. She called it the Old Religion. It didn't have anything to do with riding broomsticks or selling your soul to the devil, but Madeline was convinced that she had some magical powers. We all went along with the act. Madeline was the star, after all, and if she'd decided that we were all going to paint ourselves purple, we'd all have done it. We became members of the coven. Estelle DuBarry and Lurine Hazel and Janet Pierce and even poor, dull Clara Adams—witches one and all."

"And Jefferson Long?" said Jupe.

"Sure," said Farber. "I don't suppose he'd like it known today. He's got kind of a stuffy image on his television show. But he was a witch."

Jupiter smiled. "Do you keep in touch with any of those people?"

"With some of them," said Farber. "Jefferson Long speaks only to policemen these days, so nobody keeps in touch with him. Poor little Estelle, who caused all the trouble between Madeline and Desparto, never made it to the big time. She didn't really have talent and she didn't wear well. She now looks like my grandmother and she runs a little motel in Hollywood. She's not a bad sort."

"Do you think she'd consent to be interviewed?" asked Jupe.

"Sure. She'd enjoy the attention. Hey, what are you kids doing, anyway? The project of the year for a juvenile fan magazine?"

"Well, I'm taking a course on the history of films," said Jupe, "and . . ."

"I see." Farber took the photo from Bob and studied it. "I'll give you Estelle DuBarry's address," he said. "And I've got Ted Finley's telephone number. He's a great old guy. And still working in pictures even though he must be about eighty. Mention my name when you call him."

"How about the others?" asked Bob.

"Well, Ramon Desparto is dead, of course," said Farber. "I don't know how you'd get to talk to Clara Adams. She lives with Madeline and they don't see anyone. Nicholas Fowler, the scriptwriter, is dead, too. He had a heart attack a few years back. Forget about Janet Pierce. She married a count or a duke or somebody like that and went to Europe to live and never came back. Lurine Hazel's gone, too. She married her hometown sweetheart and went to live in Billsville, Montana. And Marie Alexander—well, it's a shame about Marie."

"She's the pretty girl with the long hair, isn't she?" said Pete. "What happened to her?"

"She went swimming off Malibu one day and got caught in a riptide and drowned."

"Good grief!" exclaimed Pete. "That's three people in the coven who are dead!"

"It's been a long time since that picture was taken," said Farber. "We haven't done too badly. Now Gloria Gibbs, the plain one who was Ramon Desparto's secretary, she works for a broker out in Century City. Every once in a while I take her out to dinner."

Jupiter took the photo and looked at it again. He pointed to the man who was identified in the caption as Charles Goodfellow. He was a very thin young fellow with dark hair that was slicked back. "He looks familiar," said Jupe. "Is he still working in films?"

Farber frowned. "Goodfellow? I'd almost forgotten about him. He did bit parts back in the old days—you know, playing taxi drivers and doormen. You've probably seen him if you watch a lot of old movies on TV. I don't know what happened to him. He's the only one I've completely lost track of. He's one of those people who are easy to forget. About the only thing I remember is that he was American, but for some reason his parents lived in Holland when he was a child. He was kind of a pill. Very fussy. He almost had a fit when he found out that we were all supposed to sip honey and water out of the same cup at the Sabbats. He used to do it, but he always went and gargled afterward."

The three boys laughed. "You make a witch's coven sound as sinister as a square dance," said Jupiter.

"It was all very innocent," said Farber. "Only, after Desparto died, some of the people began to wonder whether Madeline didn't, in fact, have some power."

"She put a curse on Desparto?" asked Jupiter.

Farber sighed. "Maybe I shouldn't tell you. It was . . . well, the sort of thing people say when they're very angry. She told him to go hang himself. Now that's just an expression. I'm sure she didn't mean it. Only right after she'd said it, Ramon Desparto climbed into his car and drove away—and the brakes failed so that he drove into a tree. There were no seat belts in those days, and he was thrown clear of the car. We found him wedged in the crotch of a tree partway down an embankment on the side of the road. He was just hanging there with his head to one side. His neck was broken."

"My gosh!" said Pete.

"So the coven broke up, and Madeline withdrew, and that was the end of that. Now no one talks to Madeline, and I guess not many talk about her."

"How about her manager? He used to be her chauffeur," said Jupe.

"Didn't really know him," said Farber. He took a piece of paper from a pad on the counter and wrote Estelle DuBarry's address on it. Then he added Ted Finley's telephone number and the address where Gloria Gibbs worked in Century City. He gave the paper to the boys, and when they left the shop he stood leaning on his counter, staring straight ahead in an unseeing fashion.

"Nice guy," said Pete, when they were outside, "and he sure likes to talk."

"Yes, even though I guess we stirred up some bad memories for him," said Bob. "He looks as if he's seeing Ramon Desparto again, hanging in the crotch of a tree with his neck broken."

11

Friends and Enemies

The motel that Estelle DuBarry managed was on a side street off Hollywood Boulevard. When Bob rang the bell outside the office, an aging woman with bleached blonde, curly hair and very black eyelashes came to the door.

"Miss DuBarry?" said Bob.

"That's right." She squinted slightly, as if she might need glasses.

"Elliott Farber told us you might be willing to talk with us," said Bob. "We're doing a paper for school. It's a summer project on the history of the motion picture."

"Why, how nice!" said the woman. "I'll be happy to talk with you." She opened the screen door and swung it wide. The boys went into a stuffy little room that was part office and part living room. They took seats, and the faded actress immediately launched into the tale of her career in films. She had come to Hollywood as a young girl, and had taken a screen test. She told them how she had been given roles in several unimportant pictures and a few important ones. And since Estelle DuBarry's career hadn't been outstanding, she soon ran out of things to say to the boys.

Jupiter mentioned Madeline Bainbridge then, and the atmosphere in the little room changed abruptly.

"That terrible woman!" cried DuBarry. "She hated me. She always hated me! I was pretty, and not so high and mighty as she was. If it hadn't been for her, I wouldn't be running this crummy motel today. If it hadn't been for her, Ramon and I would be married and living in some big house in Bel Air!"

There was shocked silence. DuBarry glared at Jupe and he looked away. "Mr. Farber mentioned a coven," he said at last. "Can you tell us anything about the coven?"

The color left Estelle DuBarry's face, then flooded back in a crimson tide. "We . . . we were just playing games, you know," she said. "We didn't believe in it. Except for Madeline. She believed in it."

"So you didn't believe in witchcraft, and you still don't?"

"Of course not!" cried the former actress.

"You said an interesting thing a few moments ago," said Jupe. "You said that if it weren't for Madeline Bainbridge, you and Ramon Desparto would be living in Bel Air today. How could that be? Ramon Desparto died in an accident."

"That was no accident!" cried the woman. "It was . . . it was . . ."

She didn't finish the sentence.

Bob moved awkwardly in his chair. "It was very nice of you to take the time to see us," he said. "Do you know of anyone else we should see—any friend of Madeline Bainbridge who might still be in touch with her? Or with her secretary?"

"I do not," said the woman.

"There was a man named Charles Goodfellow," said Jupe. "Do you know what became of him?"

She shrugged. "He just dropped out of sight."

"I see," said Jupe.

The boys left, and walked down the drive to the car, where Beefy waited.

"She doesn't know anything that can help us," said Bob.

"She thinks Bainbridge murdered Desparto," Pete put in. "I think she's really afraid of Bainbridge."

"Elliott Farber suggested as much," said Jupe. "I wonder if Ted Finley will have any information we need."

"I wonder if Ted Finley will even talk to us," said Bob.

"I imagine he will," said Jupiter. "Madeline Bainbridge is big news today, after the theft of those films. Ted Finley won't object to being associated with her."

Jupe proved to be correct. After a quick lunch, he telephoned Ted Finley from Beefy's apartment. He got an answering device, but Ted Finley called back almost immediately. The old character actor was cheerful and cooperative. He quickly admitted that there had been a coven, and that he had been a member.

However, although he expressed great admiration for Madeline Bainbridge, he denied that he was ever in touch with her.

"Nobody keeps in touch with Madeline," he said. "That chauffeur of hers—that Gray—he took over completely once Madeline retired. He always answered the telephone, and he always said she didn't want to talk to anyone. For a while after Desparto died, I tried to keep her from being a complete hermit. It didn't do any good, and after a while I gave up. Maybe things will be better, now that her pictures have been sold to television."

"And stolen," Jupe reminded him. "They're being held for ransom."

"And they'll *be* ransomed," predicted Finley. "They're priceless. Now that you young folks will have a chance to see them, I expect I'll be getting a lot of calls about Madeline."

"Just one more thing, Mr. Finley," said Jupe. "Do you know what happened to the man named Charles Goodfellow? He's the only one of Madeline Bainbridge's close friends that I haven't been able to locate."

"Goodfellow? No, can't say that I do know. He was kind of a dim young man. Maybe he went back home —wherever that might be—and got a job clerking in a hardware store or something."

Jupe thanked the actor, and Ted Finley hung up.

"Nothing," Jupe said to his friends. "He doesn't know anything and hasn't been in touch with Bainbridge for years."

"We haven't contacted Gloria Gibbs yet," Bob reminded Jupe. "You have the name of the broker she works for."

Jupiter nodded. "I'll call her, but I think we're wasting time."

In a dogged and discouraged way, Jupiter dialed the number of Gloria Gibbs's employer. The woman who answered the telephone turned out to be Gloria Gibbs herself. She was even less helpful than Madeline Bainbridge's other friends had been, and more hostile. "That was all a long time ago," she said, "and I don't feel that I'm any more important because I once knew that blonde witch."

"Yes, she was a witch," said Jupe quickly. "You were a member of her coven, weren't you?"

"Yes, and it was a big bore. I don't like staying up late just to dance around in the moonlight."

Gloria Gibbs then brusquely denied ever being in touch with Madeline Bainbridge, or with the missing coven member, Charles Goodfellow. She announced in sharp tones that Clara Adams was a poor, beaten-down creature in whom nobody would be interested, and she hung up.

"Unpleasant woman," was Jupe's comment. "However, she only confirms what others have told us. There was a coven, but if that's the sinister secret in Madeline Bainbridge's memoirs, it isn't making anyone nervous. We don't know about our missing coven member, Charles Goodfellow, but no one else is worried about witchcraft. So that's not it unless..." Jupe stopped and frowned. "Jefferson Long!" he said. "He's the only one who wouldn't admit to being a member of the coven. But he couldn't have stolen the manuscript.

He was on camera with Marvin Gray at the time the manuscript was taken."

"He could have hired somebody," Pete suggested. "And maybe Gray did mention it to him. He could even have told him it was here, and then forgotten he did it."

"It's a bare possibility," said Jupe, "but not likely. Where would Long find the time to arrange a theft while he was busy setting up an interview? Still, for some reason Long makes me uneasy. I wonder what the law enforcement people really think about him."

"You think he's a phony?" asked Pete.

"I had the impression he was playing a role," said Jupe. "He seems to know everybody in law enforcement in Southern California. If that's true, he's got to know Chief Reynolds in Rocky Beach. Let's see if the chief can give us some background on him. Somehow I'll believe the chief better than I'll believe a lot of plaques and scrolls."

12

The Man from Arson

"Jefferson Long?" Chief Reynolds leaned back in his swivel chair. "Sure, I know Jefferson Long. He shows up at every convention of law enforcement people that's held anywhere in the state."

The Chief of Police of Rocky Beach leaned forward and stared curiously at The Three Investigators. The boys sat on straight chairs across the desk from him. "Why are you interested in Long?" he wanted to know.

"I can't say exactly without betraying a confidence," Jupe told him.

"Hm!" said the chief. "That sort of talk usually means your juvenile detective firm has a client. Okay. Just so you keep out of trouble.

"I've seen Long around at meetings, and every once in a while I catch him on television. He's okay. He gives people some straight scoop on crime and criminals. Of course, he claims to be an investigative reporter. That would mean that he actually does some detective work on his own. He doesn't. In my opinion, he's just a brain-picker—he gets his information from people who have done the hard work of digging out facts. I don't even think he's all that interested in law and order. He just latched onto that as a cause; he wanted to make a name for himself and promote his crime reports on TV."

"So he's a phony," said Pete. "But how come he gets all those awards from police departments and sheriffs' offices?"

Chief Reynolds shrugged. "He does keep the public informed about things like fraud and burglary and forged money and such things. Law enforcement people want the public to trust them, and Long does encourage people to trust the police—and to call the police if they think there's anything strange going on in their neighborhoods. So the man does help us a lot that way."

"But he isn't the hotshot crime-fighter he pretends to be," summarized Jupiter. He nodded with satisfaction. "I had a feeling he was acting a role."

"He does it twenty-four hours a day," said the chief.

The boys thanked the chief, then left the police station and started hiking up the highway.

"Another dead end!" complained Jupiter. "We punctured Long's balloon, but now I'm sure that he had nothing to do with the theft of Madeline Bainbridge's manuscript."

"Why do you say that?" asked Bob.

"Because, from everything we've heard, I think Long really values his good relations with the police.

He's built a successful career on that, and I don't think he'd jeopardize his career by stealing a manuscript that would merely embarrass him."

"Then why did he lie to you about the coven?" demanded Pete.

"It's not surprising. Why should a man in his position tell a strange kid about some silly stuff in his past? And that's all it was—silly stuff, not crimes. Anyway, even if Long knew about the manuscript and wanted to steal it, he didn't have any opportunity. The timing's all wrong."

Glumly, the Investigators separated and headed for their homes. Jupiter was moody and absent-minded during dinner with Aunt Mathilda and Uncle Titus. After the dishes were done, he went to his room to lie on his bed and stare at the ceiling. He felt utterly discouraged. It seemed that there was no way to connect any of Madeline Bainbridge's old companions to the theft of the manuscript. But if none of the actress's friends had stolen her memoirs, who had?

Jupe recalled the night of the fire. Again he seemed to hear the roar as the flames licked at the timbers of the old Amigos Adobe. After they had been hauled out of the basement, he and Bob and Pete had stood across the street watching the fire. Mr. Grear had been with them, and then Beefy and his uncle had come hurrying up. Mr. Thomas had been there, too, and so had Mrs. Paulson. They, and only they, had known that the manuscript was in Beefy's apartment. Yet it seemed most unlikely that any of them would have taken it.

After a while, Jupe drifted off to sleep. When he woke, the sun was coming in the window. Still feeling frustrated and lethargic, Jupe got up, showered, and dressed. Then he telephoned Bob and Pete and arranged to meet them at the bus stop on the Coast Highway after breakfast.

It was almost nine when Jupe walked from The Jones Salvage Yard down to the highway. Bob and Pete were already there, waiting for him.

"You have any brainstorms overnight?" asked Pete.

"No," said Jupe. "I can't think of anything to do but go back to Beefy's and keep plodding along, checking on people."

"We're just about out of people we can check," Bob pointed out.

"We're out of people who had an obvious motive," said Jupiter. "We are not out of people who had an opportunity. In fact, we haven't even started on them!"

"The employees at Amigos Press?" asked Pete.

Jupiter nodded.

"I can't quite see any of them swiping that manuscript," said Pete, "but we've tried everybody else."

The three boys rode into West Los Angeles and arrived at the door to Beefy's apartment just as a slender man wearing gabardine slacks and a seersucker blazer was leaving. He smiled at the boys as he passed them in the hall.

Beefy's usually ruddy face was pale when he let them in. Behind Beefy, William Tremayne paced up and down and shouted.

"It's a conspiracy!" he cried. "They hate me! They've always hated me! Bunch of yahoos!"

"Take it easy, Uncle Will," pleaded Beefy.

"What do you mean, take it easy? You haven't been

accused of arson!"

"Arson?" cried Jupe. "The fire was arson?"

" 'Fraid so," said Beefy. "The man who just left here was from the arson squad. He wanted a list of all the employees at Amigos Press, and he wanted to know who visited the office the day the fire broke out."

"He also wanted to know to whom the insurance money would be paid," said Will Tremayne. "I know what he was *really* saying when he asked that question. He was saying that he thought I set the fire! Well, of course the insurance money will come to me. I handle all of the publishing house's financial affairs. But even if the income from my stocks *is* down . . ."

"Uncle Will, are you in trouble?" asked Beefy.

"Just a bit short of ready cash," said Will Tremayne. "Nothing important. Nothing that won't right itself in time. Now don't *you* start! It was bad enough talking to the arson investigator. I wasn't anywhere near Amigos Press when the fire started. I was here at home with you."

"Whoever started the fire didn't have to be there," said Beefy. "You heard the man. It was an incendiary device using magnesium and a battery-operated clock. It could have been put into the cupboard under the stairs anytime after six in the morning."

"You think I did it!" shouted Will Tremayne.

"I didn't say that," declared Beefy. "I only think an alibi isn't any good in this case. The arsonist was probably miles away when the fire began."

"Grear!" said Will Tremayne. "He did it! He's always hated me. Dull little mole of a man! He hates anybody who has any style. Or Thomas! What do we know about Thomas? He's only been with the firm for three months!"

"Uncle Will, *you* hired him!"

"Well, he had such good references. But that doesn't really mean anything!"

Will Tremayne went to the coffee table and snatched the lid off the box that usually contained his cigars. "Oh, blast!" he cried. "Empty!"

He glared at Beefy. "It was Grear or Mrs. Paulson," he said. "They hate me! They've never forgiven me for taking your father's place! Or it was Thomas. We don't know about Thomas. Now here's what we do. You hired these three boys to find that silly manuscript by that has-been actress. We'll just have them go and watch Grear's apartment, and Mrs. Paulson's house, and Thomas's place, too. They'll see what happens after the detective from arson visits them. I'm betting that after they're questioned, the one who did it will give himself away. He'll pack up and run. You'll see!"

Beefy looked helplessly at The Three Investigators.

"Why not?" said Jupiter. "Stranger crimes have been committed for stranger motives. If you'll give us the addresses, we'll go and stake out the three houses. It can't hurt."

"Okay." Beefy went into the small study off the living room. He was back in a minute with three addresses written on three pieces of paper.

"Now," said Jupiter, "suppose I watch Mrs. Paulson's. Bob, you can see what Mr. Grear does when he's not working. And Pete can keep an eye on Mr. Thomas."

The boys went to the door, with Beefy following

them. He came out into the hall, his face grave and concerned.

"You're just doing this to humor Uncle Will, aren't you?" he said.

"Not quite," said Jupiter. "We've checked on all the members of Madeline Bainbridge's magic circle—all that we could find, that is. As far as we can tell, none had any opportunity to take the manuscript, and none of them even knew it was here. Now we had better check the people who *did* know—and who did have the means. Any one of the three could have taken your keys from your desk and had a duplicate set made. All three were at the fire and heard where the manuscript was. Perhaps the visit of the man from the arson squad *will* stir something up. Not that I think the theft of the manuscript is necessarily connected to the fire. But we can't be sure.

"There is one thing you can do for us while we're gone," Jupe added.

"What's that?" asked Beefy.

"Your uncle says he was playing bridge with friends at the time the manuscript was taken. You could talk with his hosts and make sure this is true."

Beefy looked startled. "You suspect Uncle Will?"

"I don't know," said Jupiter. "I'd just like to have his alibi confirmed."

Beefy nodded.

"We'll meet back here after the man from the arson squad has seen our three friends," said Jupiter. The Investigators went off, leaving Beefy standing in the hall, frowning to himself.

13

The Deadly Trunk

Harold Thomas lived in a small apartment house not far from Beefy's building. There was a little park directly across the street, and Pete settled himself on a bench there, tried to ignore the children playing under the trees, and watched.

It was almost an hour before a plain dark sedan parked in front of Thomas's building. The man in the seersucker blazer got out of the car and went into the apartment house.

Pete didn't move, but his heart beat a little faster.

The investigator from the arson squad wasn't in the apartment more than fifteen minutes. Pete saw him come out and get into his sedan and drive away. Still Pete waited.

Half an hour after the detective had left, Harold Thomas came out and glanced up and down the street. He hesitated, looked back at the apartment, then turned south toward Wilshire and strode briskly away.

When Thomas was half a block from the apartment, Pete began to follow him, walking on the opposite side of the street. He tailed Thomas south, across Wilshire, and soon reached a dismal little area where small industrial buildings were clustered together. There were a few apartments, but these were shabby little places with peeling paint and torn screens.

Harold Thomas stopped in front of one of these run-down houses and looked up and down the street. Pete ducked out of sight behind a parked car.

After a moment, Thomas crossed the street and went in through the open gate of an auto wrecking yard. He stopped briefly at a shed which stood beside the gate, then went on. Through the cyclone fence that enclosed the yard, Pete saw him threading his way past heaps of rusting auto bodies and rows of mechanical parts.

Pete frowned, wondering if he should attempt to follow Thomas. Then he decided that if Jupiter had been in his place, he would keep tailing the prim accountant. If there was someone in the shed at the entrance to the yard, Pete would make up a story in grand style—just as Jupiter would. He would say that he was looking for the transmission from a 1947 Studebaker Champion.

But the shed at the gate was empty. Pete went on into the yard, moving carefully and quietly around the stripped-down auto bodies and the piles of rusting used parts.

Suddenly Pete stopped still where he was. He had heard a car door open.

The tall boy listened intently. There was a tinny

clanking—the sound of pieces of metal hitting together. It came from off to his left. It seemed to be just on the other side of a pile of fenders.

Pete crept forward and peered around the fenders. He held his breath. Harold Thomas was not five feet away. He stood next to a gray van that was parked in a clear area in the very center of the yard. The rear doors of the van were open, and inside the vehicle were piles and piles of film cans. Pete had seen cans of motion picture film many times when he visited his father at the studio where Mr. Crenshaw worked. Now Pete stared at the cans, trying to read the labels on their rims. He made out "Cleopatra—Reel I" on one label. Another was marked "Salem Story—III." The wrecking yard seemed suddenly still. There was only the roar of blood in Pete's own ears and the beating of Pete's own heart.

Then Harold Thomas slammed the doors of the van. He walked to the front of the vehicle, climbed behind the wheel, and started the engine. A moment later the van was rolling up the rutted dirt drive that led to the gate.

Pete stayed where he was for a second, stunned by what he had seen. The film cans! It seemed impossible —unbelievable—but it had to be true. Those had to be the films that had been stolen from the laboratory next to Amigos Press. And Harold Thomas had them!

Pete forced himself to move. He ran, not worrying now about caution. At the gate of the salvage yard he was in time to see the van heading north. He tried to read the license plate, but he couldn't. Whether by accident or not, the plate was too dusty.

Pete ran to the door of the shack near the gate. He saw a desk and a couple of battered chairs—and a telephone. He took Beefy's telephone number out of his wallet with shaking fingers, and dialed.

The telephone at the other end rang once, twice.

Outside the shed, someone was walking on the hard earth that had been packed down by the passage of hundreds of cars and trucks. Pete did not look around. If the owners of the yard objected to his using the telephone, he would simply say that he had to call the police.

Beefy answered at the other end of the telephone.

"Beefy, listen," said Pete quickly. "This is Pete and I'm at an auto salvage yard on Thornwall, two blocks south of Wilshire. Tell Jupe and Bob that I just saw . . ."

A shadow fell across the desk, and Pete started to turn toward the door of the shed. But something crashed into the back of his neck. Then the light was gone and the telephone clattered to the floor, and Pete was falling . . . falling . . . falling!

Pete didn't know how long he was unconscious, but when he came to his senses he was in a close, dusty place—a place that smelled of grease and old rubber. It was hot—terribly hot—and it was dark. Pete tried to move, to turn over or stretch out, but he couldn't. There was no room for him to straighten himself. His neck hurt, and there was something hard pressing down on his shoulder. His hands touched metal surfaces that were rough, as if they had been eaten away by rust and time. Pete realized that he was probably still in the wrecking yard. He was locked in the trunk of some old car, and the sun was beating down on it, turning it into an oven.

Pete tried to shout, but his throat had gone dry with heat and fear. He closed his mouth and tried to swallow. There was silence outside in the yard. No one was there. No one would come to help him. He felt a surge of panic. No one would ever come!

14

The Mysterious Second Man

Beefy's car roared down the street, then screeched to a stop at the entrance of the wrecking yard. Bob and Jupe tumbled out and darted into the office.

Bob looked wildly around the empty shack. "Where is he?" he said. "This has got to be the place. It's the only wrecking yard near here."

Beefy stumbled through the doorway. "There's a man coming," he reported. "He looks as if he might work here."

The boys went to the door. A man with thick, curly black hair was striding up the drive, coming from some far corner of the yard. He wore coveralls that were stained with grease. "Anything I can do for you folks?" he said cheerfully when he saw Beefy and the boys at the office.

"We're looking for a friend," Jupe told him. "He

said he'd meet us here. Have you seen a boy about our age? A tall boy who's muscular and rugged-looking?"

"Sorry," said the man. "Haven't seen anyone like that today."

"But he must have been here!" said Jupiter. "Are you sure you didn't see him?" In spite of himself, Jupe's voice went up. It was rough now with fear and anxiety.

"I haven't seen anybody," insisted the man. "Now look, kid, I'm sorry if you missed your friend, but this is a wrecking yard, not a hangout for kids. And I can't be at this gate nonstop. Hey! Hey, where do you think you're going?"

"Pete's here!" declared Jupe. He had darted past the salvage man and stood in the drive staring at the yard—at mounds of heaped-up auto parts, fenders and doors and engine blocks and rims—and at mountains of balding tires. "He saw something. It was something important, and he called. And somebody got to him before he could give us the message. He's here. I know it!"

Bob started suddenly and touched Jupe's shoulder. "The trunk of one of these wrecks," he said. "If I had to get rid of somebody quickly, that's where I'd put him!"

The man scowled at the two boys. "You kids are crazy!" he said, but there was an edge of doubt in his voice. "Nobody'd put your friend in one of those cars. Hey, you're kidding me, aren't you?"

"Pete!" Jupe shouted. "Pete! Where are you?"

There was no answer.

"You're not kidding, are you?" said the man, after a second. He stared about at the acres of rusting, ruined cars. "There must be about a hundred cars here that still have their trunk lids," he said. "It could take all day to find the right one."

"No," said Jupiter firmly. "If he's hidden in one of these old cars, we can get to him quickly."

Jupiter began to walk through the jumble of auto bodies. He stepped along purposefully, his eyes darting to one side and then the other. Beefy and Bob trotted after him, and the man in the coveralls trailed behind, looking worried. "That kid—your pal—he could be having heat prostration if he's locked up in one of these things."

Jupe didn't answer. He had stopped beside the body of an old blue Buick. He pointed. There was a thick coat of dust over the remains of the auto, but on the lid of the trunk there was a place where the dust had been disturbed and the paint showed through, clear and still fairly blue.

"Was that trunk lid open before now?" demanded Jupe.

"It . . . it could have been," said the man.

"Get a crowbar, will you?" said Jupe. "I think someone saw the open trunk lid, shoved Pete inside, then slammed the trunk shut, disturbing that dust!"

The salvage man didn't question Jupe now. He disappeared briefly, then returned with a crowbar. He jammed the tool in under the trunk lid. Then he and Beefy both leaned on the crowbar. Metal groaned as the trunk lid was forced open.

"Pete!" Bob darted forward.

Pete lay curled in the trunk. He didn't stir.

"Good night!" The salvage man raced off toward the

office. He returned in seconds with a towel which was soaked and dripping.

Pete was sitting up by this time, with Jupiter supporting him on one side and Bob on the other.

"Okay," he said. His voice was barely a whisper. "I'm okay. Just hot in there. Not enough air."

"Take it easy, kid," said the man. He dabbed at Pete's face with the towel. "I'm going to call the cops! I could have wound up with a corpse in one of my cars!"

"Pete, what happened?" said Jupiter.

Pete took the towel and held it to his face. "I saw Harold Thomas leave his apartment and come here," he reported. "I tailed him. There was a gray van parked here among the wrecks. He opened the back doors and looked in. It was full of film cans."

For an instant no one spoke.

Then Bob said, "Holy cow!"

"The Bainbridge films!" exclaimed Beefy. "Harold Thomas had them?"

"Sure looked like it," said Pete. "I saw a few of the labels. After he checked the films, Thomas got into the van and drove away. That's when I tried to call you and didn't quite make it."

"So Thomas stole the films," said Jupe. "He could have set the fire, too, to draw attention away from the robbery at the film laboratory."

"He must have noticed you as he drove away," said Bob. "He came back and bopped you while you were trying to make your telephone call."

"No." Pete frowned, remembering the incident. "It wasn't him. The guy who hit me didn't come from the street. He was walking toward the office from some-place inside the wrecking yard."

Bob's eyes went to the man in coveralls.

"Oh, no!" cried the man. "It wasn't me! I don't know what all this is about, but it wasn't me. I wouldn't hit anybody. Listen, I've got kids of my own. I find kids poking around here, I just yell at them and chase them over the fence!"

"I believe you," said Jupiter. "But if Pete is sure it wasn't Harold Thomas, there had to be another man."

"Thomas's confederate," declared Bob. "Remember, there were two holdup men who stole the films."

"Clever of them to hide the van with the films here, where there are hundreds of other vehicles," said Jupe. "But they took a terrible chance." Jupe looked at the owner of the yard. "You could have started stripping it, or . . ."

"The gray van?" said the man. "No. I wouldn't touch that gray van. A guy was paying me to let him park it here."

"Oh?" said Jupiter.

The man looked terrified. "Something stolen in it?" he said. "I didn't know there was any stolen property involved. I run a clean operation. There aren't any hot cars on my lot. Listen, are you guys going to call the police?"

"Do you want us to?" said Jupe.

"They'll never believe me," said the salvage man. "I don't know anything about stolen property, but they'll never believe me. This guy came driving in in that gray van, see. He's about so tall, with dark hair slicked back."

"Thomas," said Beefy.

"That wasn't his name," declared the salvage man. "He had a funny name. Puck. Mr. Puck, that's what it was. He said he didn't have anyplace to park his van at home. He said he couldn't park it on the street in front of his house because he's in a two-hour parking zone, and he'd get ticketed. So he wanted to know if he could leave the van here in the yard. I know that sounds kind of screwy now that I hear myself saying it, but it sounded okay then. So I figure, what the heck? It's ten extra bucks a week. Why not?"

"Because he's a crook, that's why not!" said Bob.

"Okay, okay. How was I supposed to know that?"

"Never mind," said Jupiter. "It doesn't matter now. And let's not notify the police. They wouldn't believe any of us. What we have to do now is get evidence."

"The stolen films are evidence," declared Pete. "Good solid evidence!"

"True. But Thomas has had time to hide them someplace by now. Maybe . . . maybe if we can get into his apartment, we can find something else that would be incriminating."

Pete stood up and took a step or two, as if testing his legs.

"You okay?" said Bob anxiously. "Are you going to be well enough to go with us?"

"Yes. I'm okay now."

"Then let's go," said Jupe. "Only let's be careful. Thomas could have been warned by now. He could be waiting for us."

"And there's that second man," said Bob. "We know he exists. We'd better watch out for him."

15

The Vanishing Suspects

"I'm going in with you," said Beefy Tremayne after he pulled to the curb in front of Harold Thomas's apartment building.

"Fine," said Jupiter, looking appreciatively at Beefy's broad shoulders. "We may need all the muscle we can get. Anyone who would put Pete into the trunk of that car and leave him there is bound to be dangerous."

The Three Investigators and Beefy went up the walk and into the vestibule of the little apartment house. There were only four doors in the entryway. One of them had a nameplate beside the doorbell that said "Harold Thomas."

Beefy rang the bell firmly. "Thomas?" he called. "Are you there?"

No one answered.

Jupiter put his hand on the doorknob and turned it.

"Careful," said Bob in a low voice. "These guys are

dangerous. You said it yourself."

Jupe pushed the door wide, and the boys and Beefy looked into a living room that was quiet and orderly to the point of being bare.

"Mr. Thomas?" called Jupe. He walked through the living room and peered into an immaculate kitchen. The others followed him, and they explored the little square hall between the living room and the bedroom, then went into the bedroom.

A closet door stood open. Except for a number of empty hangers, the closet was empty.

"Too late!" said Jupe. He went to the dresser and pulled open one drawer after another. They were all empty.

"He's gone!" said Bob.

Jupe looked at his wrist watch. "It's almost two hours since Pete saw him drive away. The second man had plenty of time to warn Thomas. Thomas and his confederate hid the films somewhere. Then Thomas came back here, packed up, and left."

Beefy stood awkwardly and watched while the boys searched the apartment. They found nothing—nothing but immaculate emptiness.

"We knew Harold Thomas was a tidy man," said Jupe at last. "He's also extremely well organized. With almost no warning, he's been able to clear out of here and not leave a trace. Well, that only makes sense. The theft of the Bainbridge films was well organized. It took place on the very day the films were delivered, and at a time when there was no one in the laboratory except one technician. Just by sitting in his office and looking across to the building next door, Thomas could have learned the routine there. But how did he know that the films were going to be sold to Video Enterprises, or that they'd be delivered to that laboratory?"

Jupiter turned to Beefy. "Did Thomas have much contact with Marvin Gray when Gray came into your office?"

"No. None that I know of."

"Hm!" Jupe's eyes were fixed on the floor next to the sofa. He bent and picked up something. "Just about the only thing in this apartment to show that Thomas was ever here," he said, and he held up a matchbook for the others to see. "The table next to the sofa is wobbly. Thomas must have jammed this matchbook under the leg to steady it."

"Just what you need!" said Bob in a mocking tone. "In the Sherlock Holmes stories, the great detective finds a collar button and immediately he can tell all about the suspect, including the fact that he was born in Ireland and that he likes kippers with his tea. You have a matchbook which is doubtless a priceless clue. Tell us about Harold Thomas!"

Jupe turned the matchbook over in his hands, and there was a strange smile on his face. "It's from the Java Isles Restaurant," he said. "From the address, I'd say that's quite near Amigos Press. In fact, Thomas could have been having dinner there the night of the fire. Except that of course he stopped first to rob the film vault."

"So?" said Pete.

"The Java Isles is an Indonesian restaurant," said Jupiter. "And suddenly it all fits together! When Harold Thomas persuaded that man at the auto wrecking yard to let him park the van there, he said his name was Mr. Puck. There's a character in Shakespeare called Puck. He's a sprite who goes around making trouble, and he has a second name. It's Robin Goodfellow!"

"Goodfellow?" cried Bob. "Charles Goodfellow was one of Madeline Bainbridge's magic circle!"

"Right!" said Jupiter. "The missing member of our coven. We know that Charles Goodfellow was raised in Holland, and many Dutch people are fond of Indonesian food because Indonesia was once a Dutch colony. Harold Thomas was also fond of Indonesian food, since he patronized the Java Isles Restaurant."

"Wow!" said Pete. "Harold Thomas is the same person as Charles Goodfellow! He was a member of the coven and he knew everybody."

"And how did he learn about the sale of the films? Which member of the coven told him? Or did he just happen to know someone at Video Enterprises? Jefferson Long, or someone else entirely? We can speculate on that all day without getting an answer. But we do know he stole the films."

"Maybe he swiped the manuscript, too," said Bob. "He knew where it was and he could have had a set of keys. He could have duplicated a set from the ones Beefy kept in his desk at the office."

"He could have set the fire, too," said Pete.

"But why would he take the manuscript?" wondered Beefy. "How could that manuscript hurt him?"

Jupiter shrugged. "Who knows? Madeline Bainbridge may have written something that would expose him, even after all these years."

"I think we'd better call the police," said Beefy. He stood up. "It will be awkward explaining to them how we know all the things we know, but we have to call them. The Bainbridge films are involved, and they're of inestimable value. I think we'd better call them from my apartment. We don't really have any right in here, you know."

During the short drive to his home, Beefy grew more and more excited. "This will be a load off Uncle Will's mind!" said Beefy as he let himself and the three boys into the apartment. "We can definitely tie Thomas in with the theft of the films, and if the police can turn up some solid evidence to tie him in with the fire, Uncle Will is off the hook!"

Beefy went through the apartment, calling to his uncle. There was no answer.

"That's funny," said Beefy. "He left here right after you left this morning. He said he was going to play golf. He ought to be back by now."

Suddenly uneasy, Beefy went into his uncle's bedroom. The boys in the living room heard a closet door open, and then heard a thumping and a clattering as Beefy knocked several things over.

After several minutes, Beefy appeared again in the living room. "He's gone," he said. "He must have come back here while we were out and packed a small suitcase. There's one missing. He's . . . he's panicked and he's running. Now we can't call the police. They'll think he *did* set that fire."

"They often do think that, when suspects vanish," said Jupiter, "and are we sure—are we really sure— that he didn't?"

16

The Sleeping Beauty

"Just before we left here this morning, I asked you to call the people who played bridge with your uncle the night the manuscript was taken," said Jupiter to Beefy.

"I did," Beefy replied. The young publisher looked haggard. "Uncle Will didn't arrive for the bridge game until almost ten-thirty. He said there'd been a minor accident on Beverly Drive and he'd been held up in traffic."

"So he could have set the fire at Amigos Press, and he also could have taken the manuscript from this apartment," said Jupe.

Beefy nodded. "I can't imagine Uncle Will as an arsonist, and yet he did have a motive. He was short of money. But why on earth would he steal the Bainbridge manuscript?"

Jupiter scowled and pulled at his lower lip—a sign

that he was thinking furiously. "Could there be something damaging about *him* in that manuscript? Did he know Madeline Bainbridge when he was younger? Maybe that's why he always speaks of her so scornfully!"

Jupiter thought some more, then sighed. "No matter which way we turn, we keep coming back to the mysterious Madeline Bainbridge. Only she knows what's in her manuscript, and only she could tell us who might want it suppressed. We've just *got* to talk to her—and we have to talk to her when Marvin Gray isn't around. For whatever reason, he's too obstructive."

"But how do we reach her?" asked Beefy. "She doesn't answer the telephone. She doesn't go out. Perhaps she doesn't even open her own mail."

"You can call Gray and set up a lunch date," Jupe suggested. "Tell Gray you have something important to discuss with him and it has to be over lunch. Then pick a good restaurant and make sure the lunch lasts a couple of hours. That will give us time to get to Madeline Bainbridge."

"But . . . but what'll I discuss with Gray?" said Beefy.

"Someday you're going to have to tell him about the missing manuscript," said Bob.

"But . . . but you were going to get it back!"

Jupiter shook his head. "It's been gone for three days, and few things are easier to destroy than a manuscript. We are probably not going to get it back, and sooner or later Marvin Gray will have to be told. You can call him now and ask him to meet with you to discuss something very important."

Beefy groaned. "Okay. I'll do the best I can."

Beefy went into the den to make the telephone call. When he came back into the living room a few minutes later, he said, "Okay. I'm meeting Gray tomorrow at twelve-thirty at the Coral Cove in Santa Monica."

"Good," said Jupiter.

Pete was scowling. "You're so sure we're going to get in to see Madeline Bainbridge," he said. "Maybe she doesn't answer the door when Gray's not around. Or maybe that Clara Adams will block you. And don't forget there's a dog there—a big Doberman!"

"I haven't forgotten anything," said Jupiter. "I think we can see Madeline Bainbridge—if we're determined enough."

But at noon the next day, even Jupiter had some qualms. He and Pete and Bob had ridden their bicycles up the Coast Highway, and then had taken the paved mountain road to the turnoff a quarter of a mile from Madeline Bainbridge's front gate. There they took shelter with their bikes amid the oleanders that grew raggedly on the edges of Bainbridge's fields.

"We'll see Marvin Gray when he drives down to the highway," said Jupe to his friends. "Let's hope that he doesn't let the dog out onto the grounds before he goes. If he does and we meet the dog, we'll just stand still and call for Madeline Bainbridge to come and rescue us."

He looked out from behind the oleanders. A car was turning onto the road from the Bainbridge ranch.

"Here comes Gray," said Bob.

A dark gray Mercedes swept past the boys, throw-

ing up a cloud of dust. When it had disappeared
down the road toward the highway, Jupiter, Pete, and
Bob pushed their bikes out onto the gravel road. They
pedaled through the gate and up through the lemon
grove. The dog did not appear, but when the boys
reached the house and got off their bicycles a frantic
barking began inside the house.

"Oh, great!" moaned Pete.

They went up the steps to the porch and Jupiter
rang the bell. They heard it buzz angrily somewhere
in the back of the house. They waited.

When no one came, Jupiter rang the bell again.
"Miss Bainbridge!" he shouted. "Miss Adams! Please
open the door!"

The dog began to leap at the door. The boys could
hear him clawing at the wooden panels.

"Let's go, huh?" said Pete.

"Miss Bainbridge!" called Jupiter.

"Who is it?" cried a voice on the other side of the
door. "Quiet, Bruno! Good boy!"

"Miss Adams?" said Jupiter. "Miss Adams, please
open the door. My name is Jupiter Jones and I have
something important to say to you."

There was a fumbling with the locks. The door
opened a few inches, and a pair of faded blue eyes
looked out in sleepy wonder. "Go away," said Clara
Adams. "Don't you know you're not supposed to ring
this doorbell? No one rings this doorbell."

"I have to see Miss Bainbridge," said Jupiter. "I'm
from her publisher."

"Publisher?" echoed Clara Adams. "I didn't know
that Madeline had a publisher."

Clara Adams stepped back, letting the door open wide. Her hair straggled around her face and her eyes, which looked full at Jupe, did not really seem to see him.

"Miss Adams?" said Jupe. "Are you all right?"

She blinked sleepily, and the dog growled.

"Could I ask you to shut the dog up someplace?" said Jupe. "He's . . . he's making us all nervous."

Clara Adams took the dog's collar and, walking unsteadily, led him back to the kitchen, where she shut him in. Then she came back into the hall. "Madeline?" she called. "Where are you, Madeline? Come here, please. There are some boys here to see you."

Jupe looked around. He saw the living room, with its austere wooden chairs. He saw the dining room, and its backless benches. He listened, but he heard no sound except the slow ticking of the clock in the living room. "This place is like an enchanted castle," he said. "Nothing moves here, does it? No one comes or goes."

"Comes or goes?" said Clara Adams in her drowsy, rusty voice. "Who should come? We don't see anyone any more. Once we were very lively here, but no more. And when Marvin isn't here . . ." She stopped and seemed to be puzzling something out. "What happens when Marvin isn't here?" she said. "Hard to remember. He's always here. Only where is he now?"

"She acts as if she's been drugged," Pete whispered to Jupiter.

"She certainly does," agreed Jupe. He turned to

Clara Adams. "Where is Madeline Bainbridge?" he demanded.

Clara Adams waved vaguely, then sat down on a chair and began to doze off.

"Something's fishy here!" exclaimed Bob.

The three boys searched then, peering into all the rooms on the first floor. It was Pete who was the first to run up the stairs to the second story. In a big corner bedroom with windows that looked out toward the sea, he found Madeline Bainbridge. She was lying on a homespun coverlet on a big wooden bed. She wore a long brown gown, and her hands were folded on her bosom. Her face was very quiet. It seemed for an instant that she wasn't even breathing.

Pete touched her on the shoulder. "Miss Bainbridge?" he said softly.

She didn't stir. Pete shook her, and called her name again—and again. Jupe's words went through his mind. An enchanted castle where nothing moved. And here was the sleeping beauty in the castle.

But why didn't she wake? Why didn't she answer him?

"Jupe!" shouted Pete. "Bob! Come quick! I found Madeline Bainbridge, but I'm . . . I'm not sure I found her in time!"

17

Conspiracy!

"Maybe we'd better call the paramedics," said Bob.

"Hold it," said Pete. "She's coming around."

Madeline Bainbridge made a small, protesting sound. Then she opened her eyes, which were glazed and blurry with sleep.

"Miss Bainbridge, I made some coffee," said Bob. "Try to sit up and drink some."

"Madeline, dear!" Clara Adams sat down on the bed, holding her own cup of coffee. "Do wake up. These young men seem so concerned. I don't understand it, but they say Marvin gave us something to make us sleep."

The actress pulled herself up so that she was sitting on the bed. In a dazed fashion she took the cup of coffee that Bob held out to her. She sipped a little, making a wry face as she did so. "Who are you?" she said groggily to the boys. "What are you doing here?"

"Drink your coffee and we'll tell you," said Jupiter. "You need to be awake to hear our story."

When Madeline Bainbridge looked more alert, Jupiter started explaining. "We work for Beefy Tremayne," he said. "We're trying to help him find your manuscript."

"My manuscript?" said Madeline Bainbridge. "What manuscript? I don't understand."

"Your memoirs, Miss Bainbridge," said Jupe.

"My memoirs? But I haven't finished my memoirs. Why, I know you boys! You're the ones who came down the hill the other night when we were having our . . . our . . ."

"You were celebrating the Sabbat," said Jupiter. "We know all about it, Miss Bainbridge."

Jupe then held out a pill bottle to the actress. "We found this in the bathroom off the back bedroom. It's sleeping medicine of some sort. We think Marvin Gray put it in something you ate or drank to make sure you wouldn't answer the door or the telephone while he was away."

The actress looked at the little vial. "Drank?" she said. "We drank some tea that Marvin made for us."

"Has it happened before, do you think?" asked Bob.

"Several days ago I fell sound asleep in the middle of the afternoon. It was very odd. Clara slept all afternoon, too."

"Probably the afternoon Gray brought the manuscript in to Beefy Tremayne," said Jupe.

"You keep prattling on about a manuscript, and

about a person named Beefy Tremayne," said Madeline Bainbridge. Her voice was strong and assured now. "What exactly are you talking about?"

Jupiter told her then, with Bob and Pete chiming in from time to time to add details. The boys told of Gray's delivery of the memoirs to Amigos Press. They told about the fire at the publishing house, and about the theft of the manuscript from the Tremayne apartment.

"Your signature is on the contract for the publication of your memoirs," said Jupiter. "A forgery, I presume."

"Certainly," said Madeline Bainbridge. "I never signed a contract. And my memoirs are still here in this house. I worked on them only last night. Look in that big chest at the foot of the bed."

Pete opened the chest and the boys looked. There was a thick heap of papers, all handwritten.

"Marvin Gray must have copied them by hand," said Bob. "Then he delivered the copy to Beefy Tremayne. And then what? Did he arrange to have it stolen, perhaps by Charles Goodfellow?"

"Goodfellow?" said Madeline Bainbridge. "Don't tell me that little thief is still in town!"

"So you know Goodfellow is a thief," said Jupe.

"I know he was one. I caught him trying to take a diamond necklace out of my dressing room on the set of *Catherine the Great*. I was going to call the police, but he persuaded me he'd never do anything like that again. Then later I found out he'd been going through the women's purses while we were filming *The Salem Story*."

"A real sneak thief," said Bob. "Did you put any-thing about that in your memoirs?"

"I may have. I think I did mention it."

"That would have given him a motive. Even though he wasn't using the same name, he might be afraid he'd be found out. And with the theft of the films from the laboratory—"

"What films?" said Madeline Bainbridge.

"Your pictures that were sold to Video Enterprises," said Jupe. "Did you know that the negatives of all your films had been sold to television, or is that some-thing that Marvin Gray engineered while you were asleep, too?"

"Oh, no! I knew all about the sale of the films. Marvin handled the negotiations, and I signed a con-tract. But you say the films were stolen?"

"They were, from a laboratory next door to Amigos Press, just before the fire started. They're being held for ransom. No doubt they're safe enough, and no doubt the ransom will be paid. Did you know that Jefferson Long came out here the night of the theft to interview you? He does a TV series on law and order."

"No!" exclaimed Madeline Bainbridge. "Is that who was here? Marvin just told me that he had some busi-ness clients coming by. I stayed out of the way, as usual. I pay Marvin to deal with the outside world."

"You were keeping out of sight the next afternoon, too, when Beefy and I came here," said Jupe. He shook his head. "Miss Bainbridge, you've put yourself into a dangerous position, having no contact at all with anyone outside this house."

The actress sighed. "I let Marvin handle everything for me. It begins to look as if he handled it too well, doesn't it?"

"He must intend to swindle you out of the advance from Amigos Press for your manuscript," said Jupiter.

"That scoundrel!" said the actress. "I can't believe it!" Then she stopped and thought for a moment. "Yes," she said, "I can believe it. He was always greedy. But to think he's been deliberately withholding information and using drugs on me! Ugh! It's horrible!"

"Wouldn't it be interesting to see how much he's swindled you, and what he plans for the future?" asked Jupe. "Why not play along with him? Pretend to be asleep when he comes home today, then watch him. I'll give you a telephone number where we can be reached—a couple of numbers, in fact."

"Oh, Madeline, let's do it!" said Clara Adams. "I've always wanted to play a joke on Marvin. He's so grumpy and serious all the time."

"It will be a marvelous joke," said Madeline Bainbridge. "I can't think of a single reason why I should trust you boys, and yet I do. I have to see exactly what Marvin is up to."

"It could be almost anything," said Bob. He held up a bright orange matchbook. "I found this in a jar with a lot of other matches when I lit the stove to make coffee. It's from the Java Isles, that restaurant where Harold Thomas ate."

"So Gray and Thomas probably were in touch," said Jupe. "Gray could have been involved in some way with the theft of the films, with the theft of the manuscript, and even with the fire at Amigos Press."

"Isn't this fun?" said Clara Adams. "Like those nice old-fashioned movies where the heroine helps the detectives. We're going to nail him!"

18

The Search

It was almost four when The Three Investigators rode up in the elevator to Beefy's apartment. They found the young publisher pacing and brooding.

"How was your lunch?" Bob inquired brightly.

"As lunches go, it wasn't bad," said Beefy. "But it was a lousy business conference. I bought Marvin Gray the most expensive lunch they had at that gilt-edged beanery, and I also ordered a couple of martinis for him. He ate and drank everything, and when he began to glow like a neon sign I decided he was ready. I told him the bad news about the Bainbridge manuscript.

"Well, it didn't get to him right away. He'd been talking about Jefferson Long, and how tickled he was that Long was the one assigned by the television station to interview Madeline Bainbridge after her films were stolen. Then Bainbridge couldn't see him.

Gray really enjoyed that. Gray doesn't like Long a bit. I guess Long was uppity to him in the old days, when Gray was just a chauffeur.

"How interesting," said Jupiter.

"It gets more interesting," said Beefy. "When Gray finally got the message that the Bainbridge memoirs were missing, he sat and blinked like a stuffed owl for a couple of seconds. Then he decided that it was all a terrible shame, but maybe not quite as terrible as I might think. He decided that maybe Madeline Bainbridge wouldn't mind writing her memoirs all over again—provided I paid her double the amount of the advance we'd agreed on when she signed the contract."

Beefy put his head in his hands and shuddered. "What a mess!" he said. "I've got to get going again on Amigos Press. I've got to rent an office and get the staff together and go to work. But it's all going to take money, and I don't have any money without Uncle Will. Maybe I don't have any money even *with* Uncle Will, because if he shows up here he may be charged with arson. And the insurance company sure isn't going to pay him for burning down his own property. And then Gray tells me I should double the advance I pay Madeline Bainbridge!"

Beefy looked up at the boys. "I hope that very expensive lunch wasn't a total waste of time," he said. "Did you manage to talk with Madeline Bainbridge?"

"We sure did. Bob wrote up a report while we were coming here on the bus."

Bob grinned and took his notebook out of his pocket. He then summarized briefly the events of the day. As Beefy listened, his woebegone expression gradually disappeared. By the time Bob finished, Beefy was grinning broadly.

"I'm off the hook!" he cried. "I don't owe any advance!"

"You do not," said Jupiter. "Also, we found evidence that Gray—as well as Thomas—dined at the Java Isles restaurant. Gray could have tipped Thomas off about the films. He could have been involved in that crime."

"He could have planted the incendiary device at Amigos Press, too," said Beefy. "He had the opportunity, as did Thomas. What a relief! Of course, we'll have to prove it. Nobody will take our word for it. Is there some way we can tie the fire to Gray, so we can clear Uncle Will? Wouldn't the arsonist have to buy magnesium for his incendiary device, for example?"

"He would certainly have to get it somewhere," said Jupe cheerfully. "Suddenly a number of things have become clear to me. Beefy, may we search your apartment?"

"Search?" Beefy sat up straight. "What for?"

"For the magnesium," said Jupiter.

"Jupe, you've got to be kidding! You can't really believe that Uncle Will set that fire. Look, I know he's not the most lovable guy in the world, but he isn't a criminal. Can you picture him hiding in a corner someplace, putting together a gadget that will go off at six o'clock and destroy my office? It isn't in character."

"I know it isn't," said Jupiter. He stood still, his

head to one side as if he were listening to voices that the others couldn't hear. "There's been something that's been bothering me about this case all along— something I've been missing. I know what it is now. It's something I saw, but I didn't see. Not at the time. As a matter of fact, there were a couple of things that I missed. We can verify them when we need to. The evidence will be there. I know it will."

"Jupe's having one of his brainstorms," said Pete, who was amused by the look on Beefy's face.

"It'll be okay," Bob assured the young publisher. "Jupe has a photographic memory, and if he's just re-calling something he heard or saw, you can bet he's recalling it *exactly*!"

"Now I'd like to search the apartment," said Jupe. "I'd like to start with your uncle's room."

"Well . . . well, I guess it's all right," said Beefy. "If it will help."

Beefy led the way to the big bedroom that had windows facing to the south. The boys followed him.

Jupe went directly to the closet, which had sliding doors that took up almost an entire wall of the room. He pulled back the doors. The boys saw dozens of neatly tailored jackets and racks of gleaming shoes.

Jupiter started to go through the pockets of the jackets. He worked quickly. After only a few minutes he said, "Aha!" and pulled a strip of metal from the pocket of a tan flannel jacket.

"Don't tell me that's magnesium!" said Beefy.

"I'm sure that any laboratory test would confirm it," said Jupe. "And now I am quite positive that your uncle didn't set the fire. He just panicked and ran. If he were guilty, he'd have taken the magnesium with him."

The telephone on the table beside the bed began to ring.

"Want to answer that?" said Jupiter to Beefy. Jupe looked almost joyful. "I gave this number to Madeline Bainbridge and asked her to call here or at Headquarters in Rocky Beach if Gray did anything unusual. Perhaps that's her now."

Beefy picked up the telephone and said, "Hello." He listened for a moment, then handed the telephone to Jupe. "It *is* Madeline Bainbridge," he said, "and she wants to talk with you."

19

Setting the Trap

Jupiter stood with the telephone to his ear, and as he listened to Madeline Bainbridge, he grinned.

"That's fine, Miss Bainbridge," he said at last. "I was hoping for something like this. Now if Gray offers you something to eat or drink tonight, just pretend to take it. And warn Miss Adams. Both of you want to be alert when Gray has his visitor. Of course, you'll pretend to be asleep.

"I think we'll be able to solve the entire series of crimes, and get proof that will satisfy the police. But there is one other person who should be there—Jefferson Long."

The telephone made muted noises which the others in the room with Jupe couldn't understand. Jupe nodded. "It won't be difficult at all," he said. "You can reach Long through Video Enterprises. He does his television series for them. Tell him that there are some things about him in your memoirs, and that you're having doubts about some of them. Say you want to go over the incidents with him because you'd hate to embarrass him in public. That will surely bring him running. Tell him to be at the house about nine."

Jupe waited, then nodded and smiled. "Fine. We'll be there, so see that the dog isn't loose."

He hung up. "Madeline Bainbridge overheard Gray making a telephone call to someone named Charlie. He told Charlie to come tonight, and he'd have the money ready for him."

"Charles Goodfellow!" exclaimed Pete.

"It seems likely," said Jupiter. "And if Madeline Bainbridge is able to get Jefferson Long to the house, we should be able to settle everything at once. I think it will be very interesting to see Long and Gray and Goodfellow all together. Who wants to come along?"

"Are you kidding?" cried Pete. "I wouldn't miss it!"

"I hope I'm invited," said Beefy.

"Certainly," said Jupiter. "I think we should bring your uncle, too. He's had a bad time, and he might appreciate seeing the situation straightened out."

"Swell," said Beefy. "How do we find Uncle Will?"

"Where does he buy his cigars?" said Jupiter.

"Huh?" said Beefy.

"Yesterday morning, just before he left here, he was out of cigars," Jupe pointed out. "From what I've seen of Mr. William Tremayne, I'd guess that he smokes something expensive and unusual. Am I right?"

Beefy nodded. "He smokes special Dutch cigars. You can't get them everywhere."

"He took his car when he left here, didn't he?"

Again Beefy nodded.

"Well, if he's driving, the cigars may not help us. But I have a feeling he isn't driving any more than he has to. He was very frightened, and he may think the police are looking for him already. But wherever he is, he's smoking. Smokers always smoke more when they're nervous. Where does your uncle buy his cigars?"

"In a little shop on Burton Way," said Beefy. "They order the brand especially for Uncle Will."

"I'm betting they've seen him in the last twenty-four hours," declared Jupiter.

In a very few minutes, Beefy and The Three Investigators were in Beefy's car, headed toward Burton Way.

"You'd better talk to the shopkeeper," advised Jupe. "He'll think it's odd if any of us start asking questions. Tell him you and your uncle had a quarrel and your uncle walked out. Ask him if he's seen your uncle."

"That sounds like some dumb soap opera," said Beefy.

"Don't worry. The man will believe you," Jupe predicted. "It sounds more likely than the truth, which is that your uncle is hiding from the police."

Beefy laughed, and he pulled to the curb in front of a small shop called The Humidor. "You coming in with me?" he asked the boys.

"You go, Jupe," said Bob. "It would look weird if all three of us went in."

Jupe and Beefy got out of the car and went into the shop, where a white-haired man in a chamois waistcoat was dusting a counter.

"Mr. Tremayne, good afternoon," said the man. "Don't tell me your uncle is out of cigars already."

"No. Uh . . . not exactly." Beefy's face was redder than usual. "He bought some cigars yesterday, did he?"

"Why, yes," said the man at the counter.

"Good," said Beefy. "We . . . uh . . . we had a quarrel yesterday, you see, and he walked out and hasn't come back. I'd like to find him and . . . uh . . . apologize. Did he . . . er . . . mention where he might be going when he was here?"

"No, he didn't."

Jupiter murmured something in Beefy's ear.

"Did he have his car with him?" asked Beefy.

"Why, I don't believe he did," said the man. "He seemed to be walking. He turned toward the right when he went out, if that's any help to you."

"That's fine," said Beefy. "Thanks very much."

He fled from the shop, tripping over the doorsill as he went.

"How you guys manage to do this sort of thing all the time, I can't imagine," he declared when they were back in the car. "My mind went blank about four times."

Jupiter was grinning. "The shopkeeper said your uncle was on foot, so there's a chance he's staying somewhere in the neighborhood. Drive down that way, slowly."

Beefy started the car. They rolled along for a short distance, with Jupe scanning the fronts of small apartment buildings and larger condominiums. Suddenly

Bob leaned forward and pointed toward a small motel on the left side of the street.

"Aha!" said Jupiter. "Exactly the sort of place Mr. Tremayne would want—ultra-respectable, and the sign in front advertises locked garages. He could get his car out of sight."

"The only garage that's closed right now is the one next to room twenty-three," said Pete.

Beefy pulled into the parking place next to the room, and an instant later he and The Three Investigators were knocking on the door of number 23.

"Uncle Will!" called Beefy. "Open the door."

There was no answer.

"Mr. Tremayne, we know you didn't set the fire at Amigos Press," said Jupe. "We're going to trap the real criminals and prove that they did it. If you want to come along and help us set our trap, you'll be welcome."

There was silence for a minute more. Then the door to room 23 swung open. "Very well," said William Tremayne. "You can come in if you want to, and we'll talk about it."

20

The Surprise Party

At dusk that evening, Beefy drove up from the Coast Highway to the Bainbridge ranch. The Three Investigators were with him, and so was his uncle. For once, William Tremayne did not seem bored. His eyes were eager, and from time to time he touched his pocket, where he carried a revolver.

There was a Mercedes parked near the porch of the Bainbridge house. Behind it was a light-colored Ford. "The Ford must belong to Harold Thomas," said Jupe. "The Mercedes is Gray's. Let's make sure that neither of them leaves here before we're ready for them to leave."

Pete smiled and tried the doors of the two cars. Neither vehicle was locked. "Very good," said Pete. He took a pair of pliers out of his pocket and went to work. In seconds he had disconnected the ignition wires, disabling both cars.

"I'll stay here and keep out of sight until Long arrives," he told the others. "Good luck."

Jupiter, Bob, and the Tremaynes started up the front steps. There was an outburst of barking. It sounded muffled and far away.

"Sounds like somebody locked Bruno in the cellar," said Bob.

"Thank goodness," exclaimed Jupe. "I don't want to meet him face to face. Not when he takes his orders from Marvin Gray."

Jupe then strode boldly across the porch and rang the doorbell.

After a moment, there were footsteps in the hall. "Who's there?" called Marvin Gray.

"I have something for Mr. Gray," said Jupe loudly.

The front door opened and Marvin Gray looked out.

"Mr. Horace Tremayne would like to talk to you," said Jupiter. "So would Mr. William Tremayne."

Jupiter stood aside, and Beefy stepped forward and planted one large foot squarely on the doorsill. "Sorry to be dropping in so late," he said, "but somehow this seemed like the right moment."

Gray drew back. "Mr. Tremayne! What is it? I'd invite you in but . . . but the ladies have retired and I don't want to disturb them."

Beefy shoved the door wide and stepped across the threshold. His uncle and the boys were close behind him.

"You've met Jupiter Jones before," said Beefy. "Jupiter is a very curious young man. Some people might even say he's nosy. We're here tonight to help him satisfy his curiosity—and mine!"

Gray retreated as Beefy and Jupiter advanced. He backed into the living room, where Harold Thomas was looking around wildly, as if trying to find a place to hide the package he held.

"That's the manuscript, isn't it?" said Jupiter. "You stole it from Beefy Tremayne's apartment the same night you burned down the Amigos Adobe."

Thomas dropped the package, which broke open and spilled loose pages across the floor. He spun around and started toward the windows.

"Stay right where you are, Thomas!" shouted Uncle Will.

Thomas looked over his shoulder and saw that William Tremayne had a gun. He stopped where he was.

Beefy picked up the manuscript from the floor. He flipped through it, stopping a few times to read a paragraph or two. Then he grinned. "This is it," he said.

Jupe went back out into the hall. "Miss Bainbridge?" he called.

"She's asleep," said Marvin Gray. "She's asleep and you'd better not wake her up. I don't know anything about that bunch of papers, or the guy who brought them here, and—"

Gray stopped talking, for Madeline Bainbridge was coming down the stairs. Her white-gold hair was done up in a knot at the nape of her neck, and on her handsome face there was a smile that was both sad and triumphant.

"Marvin," she said, with a scolding note in her voice. "You hadn't planned to see me awake, but here I am."

Her eyes went to Harold Thomas, who stood gaping. "So, Charles. It *is* you. I wish I could say that it's pleasant to see you again, but it is not."

She seated herself in the living room. Clara Adams scampered down the stairs, her faded eyes twinkling with enjoyment. She perched on a window sill behind Madeline Bainbridge.

"What is that?" asked the actress, pointing to the sheaf of papers which Beefy held.

Beefy smiled and handed the manuscript to the woman. "I'm Horace Tremayne, Miss Bainbridge," he said, "and this is the manuscript that Marvin Gray delivered to my office the day your films were stolen from the laboratory in Santa Monica."

Madeline Bainbridge looked quickly at the first page. "An exact copy of the manuscript that is upstairs in my room," she said. "How tiresome of you, Marvin, to copy my manuscript and sell it. Didn't you know you couldn't possibly get away with it? Sooner or later I'd have found out."

There was a step on the front porch, and the doorbell buzzed.

"That will be Jefferson Long," said Madeline Bainbridge. "Would you let him in, Clara?"

Clara Adams darted out of the living room. She returned in a few moments with Jefferson Long walking behind her. Long's face was stony as he looked at the group in the room. He bowed to Madeline Bainbridge.

"I didn't know you were having a party this evening," he said.

"The first one in years," said Madeline Bainbridge. "Do sit down while our young friend here—his name is Jupiter Jones, and I think you've met—tells us why Marvin Gray copied my manuscript and sold it to Mr. Tremayne. He then arranged to have it stolen. At least, I imagine that's what happened."

"That's precisely what happened," said Jupiter. "Here's the story. A certain amount of it is speculation, but I think we'll be able to verify it.

"Some time ago, Marvin Gray happened to run into Charles Goodfellow, alias Harold Thomas, in an Indonesian restaurant called the Java Isles. At this meeting, Gray learned that Goodfellow was employed by a book publishing firm. Gray has a nimble brain, and it occurred to him that he could copy the memoirs which Miss Bainbridge was writing, sell the manuscript to Goodfellow's employers, then either bribe or blackmail Goodfellow into stealing the manuscript to prevent its publication. He wanted to prevent publication because Miss Bainbridge was almost ready to find a publisher herself, and it would never do to have two publishers preparing to bring out the memoirs of the same actress.

"Gray thought he could pocket the advance that is usually paid to an author upon delivery of a manuscript. Once the counterfeit manuscript was destroyed, he could stall Beefy Tremayne for a while, and then perhaps sell the true manuscript to Beefy all over again. He was counting on the fact that Beefy would feel terribly guilty about losing the first manuscript.

"Goodfellow agreed to go along with Gray. He didn't want Gray to expose him to his employers as a person who once tried to steal a necklace from Madeline Bainbridge. First Goodfellow set Amigos Press on fire, hoping to destroy the manuscript. When he learned that he had failed, he went to Beefy's apartment and stole the manuscript. I am sure he used keys which he had duplicated from the set in Beefy's desk. I think we'll find that duplicating keys is a habit with Goodfellow, and that he had keys to the pharmaceutical firm where he used to work. That's where he got the magnesium that he used to construct the incendiary device that started the fire. Magnesium is used in pharmaceuticals. It was foolish of him to plant magnesium in William Tremayne's jacket pocket when he took the manuscript. He went too far when he did that."

Madeline Bainbridge looked up. "What about the theft of my films?" she said to Jupiter. "The counterfeit manuscript was nothing compared to that theft. They'll get a quarter of a million dollars for that one!"

"The thieves collected the ransom for the films late this afternoon, Miss Bainbridge," said Jupiter. "It was on the news at six o'clock. Video Enterprises left a package containing two hundred and fifty thousand dollars in small bills in a parking lot near the Hollywood Bowl. They were advised by telephone a short time later to recover the films from a van parked in Bronson Canyon."

Madeline Bainbridge looked surprised. "That's wonderful, but . . . but Marvin was home this afternoon!

"Marvin Gray wasn't involved in the theft of the films," said Jupe. "Charles Goodfellow was—and Jefferson Long was the mastermind."

"What?" shouted Long. "You brat! How dare you?"

"We have a witness," said Jupe. "And we can tie both Goodfellow and Long in with the missing films."

"You're crazy!" cried Long.

Jupiter didn't answer. He went out into the hall and opened the front door. "Come on in," he said.

A moment later he appeared in the living room doorway. Pete was at his side.

"Surprised?" Jupe said to Jefferson Long. "You should be. Because the last time you saw Pete, he was unconscious, and you were locking him in the trunk of a wrecked car!"

21

Crash!

"You're mad!" said Jefferson Long. "I don't have to stay here and be insulted!"

"We would all appreciate it if you'd stay," said William Tremayne, and he waved the gun in his hand.

Long sat back and folded his arms. "Very well," he said, "if you're going to use strong-arm tactics."

Beefy grinned. "Okay, Jupe. Go ahead."

"When I was in his office the other day," said Jupiter, "Jefferson Long said that he'd researched a television series on drug abuse, and that he'd found that some people employed in legitimate drug firms were involved in the illicit distribution of drugs. My guess is that in the course of his investigation, Long happened to meet Harold Thomas, who was an employee at one of these firms. Like Marvin Gray, Long recognized Thomas. He knew he had once attempted to steal a necklace from Miss Bainbridge, and that he was once known as Charles Goodfellow. Perhaps he checked up on Goodfellow. Perhaps Goodfellow had a record. He might even be a fugitive. In any case, Long could blackmail him—or at least put considerable pressure on him."

"Is that the way it was, Long?" asked Beefy.

"I have nothing to say," announced Jefferson Long.

"Thomas, was Long blackmailing you?" the young publisher asked his former accountant.

"I'll talk to my lawyer," said Thomas. "No one else."

"All right," said Jupe, undismayed. "Now at about this time, something happened which disturbed Long very much. Video Enterprises decided to purchase Madeline Bainbridge's films, and they told Long that the series on drug abuse would be canceled because the money originally budgeted for this series would be used for the films.

"No doubt Long was very bitter, especially since he had never liked Madeline Bainbridge. And it must have occurred to him that he could get back at Madeline Bainbridge and could also make a great deal of money if he could steal the films.

"Jefferson Long knew he could find out what day the films would be transferred to the laboratory in Santa Monica. Anyone at Video Enterprises could learn this. It wouldn't be any secret. Long before that day came, while the negotiations for the films were still going on, he had Harold Thomas apply for a job at the business firm closest to the laboratory. Doubtless Thomas would have accepted a much humbler position than accountant to get into Amigos Press.

"By the time the films arrived at the laboratory,

Thomas knew the routine at the film lab perfectly. He saw most of the employees leave at five that day. Then he left Amigos Press, joined Long, and they forced their way into the lab. They knocked out the technician who was there, loaded the films into a van, and drove off.

"Thomas was, of course, busier than he had planned to be, since that afternoon Marvin Gray had delivered the counterfeit memoirs from Madeline Bainbridge. Thomas had to plant his incendiary device and later, after helping to steal the films, return to Amigos Press to check on the fire. Then he had to burgle Beefy's apartment."

"You haven't a shred of evidence to back up what you're saying," declared Jefferson Long.

"But we do have evidence," said Jupiter. "I overlooked it for a long time, but when I finally remembered, everything else fell into place.

"You interviewed Marvin Gray the night the films were stolen. You said that the holdup was perpetrated by a couple of men. It was a statement that sounded perfectly correct. But there was no way you could have known that there were two men. There could have been three or four or ten—or perhaps only one. Even the police didn't know, because the technician you knocked out to get those films did not regain consciousness until the next day—hours after the interview with Marvin Gray was taped."

Jefferson Long shrugged. "I assumed that there would be at least two men."

"You might claim that," said Jupiter, "but what are you going to say about the fingerprints?"

"Fingerprints?" said Long. "What fingerprints?"

"You saw Pete follow Harold Thomas from his apartment to that auto wrecking yard in Santa Monica. No doubt Thomas was going to move the films because the arson squad was getting too close to him and making him nervous. Seeing Pete made *you* nervous. You tailed Pete, and when you realized that he had seen the van, you decided he had to be gotten out of the way. You didn't know who he was or what he was up to, but you couldn't take a chance. When he tried to call for help, you hit him on the head and stuffed him into the trunk of that old car. And when you slammed down the trunk lid, you left your fingerprints."

Jefferson Long opened his mouth to protest, and then closed it again.

"How could you!" said Madeline Bainbridge. "How could you do that to a mere boy?"

"And then there's the money," said Jupiter brightly. "The ransom for the films. It was only paid this afternoon. I would not be surprised if at least part of it is still in Thomas's car. And perhaps there's some in Long's car as well. There hasn't been time to put it in a secure hiding place. Shall we look and see what we can find?"

"No!" shouted Thomas. He lurched toward the door.

Beefy tackled him, bringing him crashing to the floor, and sat on him. The material of Thomas's suit ripped, and a wallet spilled out onto the floor, together with three key chains, all loaded with keys.

"Aha!" cried Beefy.

"I'll have the law on you!" shouted Thomas. "You don't have a search warrant!"

Gray had been standing in a corner of the room, quiet and almost forgotten. As Beefy held up the keys, Gray moved. He raced past Beefy, brushed Uncle Will to one side, and was out the front door and thundering down the steps before anyone could move.

"Marvin!" cried Madeline Bainbridge.

"He won't get far," Pete assured her. "I fixed his car so that it won't start. His and Thomas's and Long's, too. We'll just call the police and they can pick Gray up as he's hiking down the hill."

But then, from outside, there came the sound of a car engine starting.

"Oh, blast!" shouted Beefy. "That's my car! He's taking my car! I left the keys in the ignition!"

Pete raced for the kitchen and the telephone, and Madeline Bainbridge went to the window. "He'll be sorry," she said, as the car pulled away from the house. "He'll be very sorry."

Jupiter and Bob saw the car's headlights flash through the lemon grove. The car reached the road and skidded into the turn. It didn't slacken speed one bit.

"Oh my gosh!" yelled Bob.

The watchers in the ranch house heard tires screech on the road, and Madeline Bainbridge screamed.

An instant later, there was a ripping of metal and a smashing of glass as the car crashed sideways into a tree. And then there was silence—a silence that seemed deadly. Madeline Bainbridge stood with her hands to her face, her blue eyes wide with horror.

"Madeline!" Clara Adams went to her and put her arms around her. "Madeline, it wasn't your fault!" she said.

"It's like the last time. It's like Ramon all over again." And Madeline Bainbridge began to weep.

"It's only a coincidence," said Jupe.

Pete had come back into the room. "The sheriff is coming," he said. "I'll call again, and I'll ask them to send an ambulance."

Jupiter nodded as he, Bob, and Beefy headed outside to see how Gray was. "It's an unfortunate way to end things," he said, "but I think we can say that this case is closed."

22

Mr. Sebastian Declines
an Invitation

A week after the Bainbridge films were recovered by
Video Enterprises, The Three Investigators went to
visit Hector Sebastian.

"I've been looking forward to reading your notes on
this case," said the famous mystery writer as Jupiter,
Pete, and Bob took seats in Mr. Sebastian's spacious
living room.

Bob smiled and handed a file folder to Mr. Sebastian.

"Great," said the novelist. "The newspaper accounts of the recovery of the money paid for the
Bainbridge movies were intriguing, but they left out
too many important details. I was waiting to get the
real scoop from you guys."

Mr. Sebastian began to read, and did not speak
again until he had finished the last sheet of paper in
the folder.

"Incredible!" he said at last. "A woman victimized by her own guilt. She hid herself away from the world and trusted nobody."

"Nobody but the wrong man," said Pete. "He could have gone on cheating her too, if we hadn't taken the bull by the horns and gone in that afternoon to find her drugged and asleep. Her accountants are going over her finances now to see how much Gray really stole from her. Gray's in the prison ward at County–USC Medical Center. The district attorney is going to press charges once he has the full story."

"Gray's lucky to be alive," said Mr. Sebastian. "Ramon Desparto wasn't so lucky when his brakes gave out on that road. Though I still can't buy the theory that Miss Bainbridge really caused either of those accidents. I'm a big mystery fan, but believing that a witch can set up a car accident is more than I can swallow. What do you think?"

Jupiter smiled. "We'll never really know, I guess," he said. "Beefy Tremayne is convinced that Gray hit the tree simply because Gray took Beefy's car, and Beefy and all of his possessions are doomed to malfunction."

"That might cheer up Madeline Bainbridge," Mr. Sebastian told him. "She seemed upset by the idea that she might have actually hurt both Desparto and Gray."

"She's trying to get over the idea that she's to blame," Bob said, "and she's trying to use her magical powers to help Beefy overcome his clumsiness. Actually, he doesn't seem to be tripping over as many things or knocking over as many things as he used to—so maybe her magic is working."

"Also, his uncle isn't giving him such a hard time anymore," Pete reported. "Having William Tremayne looking over your shoulder would upset anybody and make them drop things."

"Something puzzled me," Mr. Sebastian added. "Did the police really find Jefferson Long's fingerprints on that smashed-up car? The one that Pete was trapped in?"

The boys grinned. "That was Jupe bluffing," Bob answered. "He was hoping Long would say something and give himself away. Actually, it was Thomas who cracked and ran—or tried to run. That was just as well. Thomas had all those keys in his pocket, and they included the keys to Beefy's apartment and the keys to the pharmaceutical company where Thomas used to work. So Jupe was right when he guessed where the magnesium came from."

"Even without that bit of evidence," Jupe continued, "the police have plenty on both Long and Thomas. The ransom money for the Bainbridge films was in the trunk of Long's car. He'd been so sure of himself that he hadn't even bothered to move it. He was promptly arrested. Now Long is out on bail, and he's finding that his friendship with law enforcement people is dead. Now they know that he was just using them—and they're furious.

"As for Thomas, whose real name actually *is* Goodfellow by the way, he's served time for a number of things, including grand larceny and arson. He tried to go straight and keep an honest job, but he simply couldn't. The pharmaceutical firm where he used to work has had an audit, and there are shortages in the accounts there. Thomas just couldn't keep away from stealing, no matter what."

"Well, now he's out of circulation," Mr. Sebastian commented.

"But Madeline Bainbridge *is* in circulation again," Bob reported. "She's decided that it's dangerous to be a hermit so she's giving a party next Friday night. She's inviting the local members of her old magic circle."

"And they're coming?" Mr. Sebastian asked in surprise. "According to your report, those women seemed to dislike Madeline Bainbridge."

"They do, but they're also curious," Jupiter said. "They want to see what she looks like after all these years—whether she has gray hair or wrinkles. So they're coming. And they'll find her so unchanged that I'm sure they'll believe that she really is a witch! A good witch, perhaps, but a witch all the same."

"I bet the simple life she's led has helped to keep her young-looking," the novelist responded.

"It's amazing how young and energetic she seems," Jupe reported. "She says she owes it all to health foods—she's eaten nothing else for more than thirty years."

"I really hope she doesn't consider deadly night-shade a health food," Mr. Sebastian commented wryly.

Jupe laughed. "No, she told us that it was reserved for use in certain Sabbat potions—in very tiny quantities, of course. By the way, you also are invited to her party if you'd like to come. We told her we were seeing you today and she says she is a big fan of your mystery novels. Would you care to dine on health foods at the ranch above Malibu? Or are you nervous about eating with witches?"

Mr. Sebastian considered this, and then he shook his head. "Please tell Miss Bainbridge for me that I'm sorry I won't be able to join her," the writer said. "I'm not nervous at all about witches—especially witches that are as attractive as Madeline Bainbridge. But when it comes to health foods—there I draw the line!"

THE THREE INVESTIGATORS MYSTERY SERIES

NOVELS

(*Continued on next page*)

FIND YOUR FATE™ MYSTERIES

The Case of the Weeping Coffin
The Case of the Dancing Dinosaur

PUZZLE BOOKS

The Three Investigators' Book of Mystery Puzzles